THE *of* Gales CHANCE

GORDON DONNELL

iUniverse LLC
Bloomington

THE GALES OF CHANCE

iUniverse books may be ordered through booksellers or by contacting:

iUniverse
1663 Liberty Drive
Bloomington, IN 47403
www.iuniverse.com
1-800-Authors (1-800-288-4677)

ISBN: 978-1-4917-1375-4 (sc)
ISBN: 978-1-4917-1376-1 (e)

Printed in the United States of America.

iUniverse rev. date: 11/05/2013

Chapter 1

*E*ARL CHILDERS DIMMED THE ROOM lamp and eased into a chair. The night-lit skyline of San Francisco spread before him, an unfamiliar vista rendered vaguely unreal by tendrils of fog drifting in from the Bay. An ornate bucket stood on a tripod beside him, provided by the hotel to chill champagne. He worked a bottle of Coca Cola loose from the ice and took a sip.

The flavor brought memories of his youth. He would pedal his bicycle out to the local golf course and spend the summer days caddying; a dollar or two and a cold Coke at the end of each round. Days of innocence, before the hazing he would endure as a bookish high-school student, before the isolation of a faraway college, before the nightmare of Vietnam. Days free of the cynicism that had come to rule the past four decades of his life. He had given them little thought until the cancer, the trial and his exile to the West Coast.

A brilliant flash startled him back to reality. The window rattled, as if thunder had followed lighting. Flames erupted from an upper floor in a nearby high-rise, shooting straight out with blow-torch intensity and then curling up the outside wall to threaten the floors above. Childers fumbled the bottle into its bed of ice.

His room was near the top of the hotel, too high for him to see the street from where he sat. Months had passed since he finished physical therapy but stamina remained elusive. He put both hands on the arms of his chair to boost himself to his feet, pausing to be sure of his balance before he made his way to the window for a better view of the burning building.

Smoke boiled out and rose into the night. Smoldering debris fell and floated toward the street below. A quick count from the sidewalk up established that the fire had originated on the eighteenth floor. No signage was visible that might identify the building. Childers returned to his chair and lifted the telephone from the side table.

The invitation he had decided to forego haunted him while the line rang. The meeting would be on eighteen. He could walk. It was only a block or so from his hotel.

"Concierge desk. May I help you?"

"I've just seen an explosion and fire," Childers said. "Can you tell me--?"

"The emergency is not in the hotel, Sir. There is no danger. We are asking that guests remain in their rooms."

"Is it the Savannah Condominium Tower?"

"Sir, there is no danger. Please remain in your room."

"This is not a curiosity question," Childers said. "It's important that I know."

"That's what someone said, but I can't confirm it. Please remain--"

"Thank you," Childers said. "Very much."

He cradled the phone. The reflections of colored strobes flickering in the glass of nearby buildings told him emergency response was arriving below. His hand could have been steadier when he lifted the phone again and pressed out a ten digit number.

"May I help you?"

A woman's voice, not recorded but with the monotone assurance of scripting. She gave no indication of whom he had reached.

"My name is Earl Childers. I was given this number by an Assistant US Attorney in Manhattan."

"May I have the last four digits of your Social Security number?"

Childers recited them from habit.

"And your mother's date of birth?"

He was surprised that he had to think to remember. He didn't recall giving the information to anyone in government.

"Are you in immediate danger, Mr. Childers?"

"No."

"I'll transfer you. Please hold."

Vapid music did nothing to calm Childers. A helicopter arrived above and upwind from the fire. Rotor downwash raised galactic swirls of smoke. Light from the aircraft's underbelly probed uncertainly into the churning haze. The uncertainty, Childers decided, was the product of his imagination, a reflection of the fact that he was calling a number he had never called before and had no idea what he should say or expect.

"Mr. Childers?" A male voice this time.

"Yes."

"How may I help you?"

"I'm in San Francisco. I just saw an explosion and fire in the Savannah Condominium Tower. On the same floor where I was invited to a meeting this evening."

"Were the explosion and fire intentional?"

"I don't know." Childers wondered if he were jumping at shadows.

"Have you received threats following your testimony?"

"No."

"Who invited you to the meeting?" the man asked.

"A bank officer named Spencer Van Wyck."

"What is your relationship with Mr. Van Wyck?"

"Business acquaintance," Childers said.

That wasn't strictly true. He and Van Wyck had no relationship beyond a few idle words exchanged at corporate receptions.

Van Wyck's call had come out of the blue. He refused to say what the meeting was about. He simply described it as critical, quickly growing impatient with Childers' questions. He seemed to view his wishes as compulsory and hung up without bothering to obtain a commitment.

"Did you plan to attend?" the man asked.

Childers explained that his absence was a last minute decision. His day had been more hectic than he expected. Warned by shortness of breath and a shambling gait that his physical reserves were depleted, he decided to remain in his hotel.

"Was Mr. Van Wyck aware of that?" the man asked.

"He didn't leave a local phone number."

"Do you have any contact information," the man asked.

Childers gave him the name of the bank where Van Wyck worked, and his position.

"Were you provided a list of security precautions following your testimony?" the man asked.

The list had been pabulum about keeping doors and windows locked, admitting no one he didn't know and avoiding unfamiliar locations. Childers had tossed it.

"I remember the guidelines," he said.

"In the event of a life-threatening emergency, dial 911," the man instructed. "For other assistance, this number is staffed 24/7."

"Thank you."

The man hung up and left Childers with no idea what, if anything, the call had accomplished. He didn't know whether the man had taken him seriously. Even if he had, supervisors who reviewed the information could dismiss it as unsupported or trivial. Childers stared out at the fire, shaken by the realization that he was a spectator at what could have been the end of his life. He rose again from his chair.

On the luggage rack lay a brass-bound leather case, about four feet long. Inside was an old Winchester, the twin of his father's treasured hunting rifle. Being allowed to fire that rifle had been a youthful rite of passage. Memories flooded back when he saw this one in a pawn shop display window.

He set the Winchester across his lap and slid four .30 caliber cartridges into the loading port. The workings were just as he remembered. Drop the lever enough to unlock the action. Push all the way forward to retract the bolt. Draw most of the way back to chamber a round. Click it up the last bit to lock the action. The ritual gave him as much comfort as the loaded weapon. He thumbed the hammer to half-cock and set the rifle aside.

The Savannah was still disgorging volumes of smoke from the upper floors, but the flames were down to brief eruptions. The building's fire suppression system appeared to have protected everything below eighteen. Childers tinkered with the TV remote until he found breaking news coverage.

The explosion and fire had pre-empted scheduled programming. The street below the Savannah Tower filled the screen, lined with emergency vehicles and lit by a surreal mix of floodlights and flashing strobes. The police had closed off the block, keeping cameras too far back to pick up the sound associated with their images. A reporter provided voice-over commentary for footage of fire crews hurrying people out of the building, escorting those who could walk and carrying one who couldn't. The commentary was more hysteria than information. Childers switched channels.

More coverage. A man and woman behind a studio anchor desk. Live feeds dancing across background monitors. Some sort of official on the phone. The blaze had already been deemed suspicious. A task force of local, state and federal investigators would be assembled, although it would require time to determine the cause. Childers shut it off and took another drink.

The Coca Cola was ice in his throat. Nostalgia had turned to nerves. He was no longer young and never would be again. A lifetime of chasing the next deal and the next dollar had left him a broken old man. His dream of a tranquil retirement had just been snatched away. He was alive only because he had been too frail to answer a summons to his death.

Chapter 2

EPUTY U.S. MARSHAL VALENTINA FLORES went through the assignment paperwork with a wary eye. Something wasn't right. This was her first day back from suspension and she was being sent straight into the field. No supervisor counseling. No psych evaluation. No requirement that she read and initial a shitload of regulations. She stopped at what appeared to be a news photo, a group emerging from an imposing building. Erect carriage and an expensive topcoat set a gaunt, older man apart.

"Who is Earl Childers?" she asked.

"Former prosecution witness," Howard Webster said. "Trial wound up last month."

Webster was a graying African-American with a rumble of authority in his voice. The excess weight of desk duty sagged from a core of muscle and wedged him between the arms of his swivel chair. His expression was pleasant and paternal, a sure sign he was hiding something.

"Shouldn't Childers be in witness protection?" she asked.

"It was a white collar prosecution. No history of violence associated with either defendant."

"Then what is this about?"

"Tina, it's a simple job. Protective surveillance."

She read aloud from the remarks section. "No contact with subject except in case of imminent physical danger. Deadly force authorized."

"It's not likely to come to that," Webster said.

"Is that what you heard from the old boy's network?"

6

Webster's face turned to stone. Thirty years in the Marshals Service had given him a career wall of framed citations and a jealously guarded spider web of contacts throughout government. She needed to tap into whatever he had learned.

"No one in the Service would write 'deadly force authorized'," she said. "Deadly force is covered by policy. You called your cronies to find out where the assignment originated."

She could feel icicles in the silence between them.

"Talk to me, Web. You're my boss. If I screw up, it's on your record too."

His shoulders moved uncomfortably. "How much do you know about private equity?"

More than she wanted to. Private equity was a snooty and secretive branch of Wall Street finance. It was also the specialty of the oh-so-handsome William A. Montgomery III, of the Maryland Montgomerys, and no amount of cleavage could distract him from talking about it over dinner. Between his career and his mirror, Bill didn't have a lot of time for romance, and his mama didn't see any room on the family tree for some Latina who packed federal tin and a .40 caliber Glock. Common sense told her it was time to give up on the situation. Emotionally, it hadn't happened.

"Private equity is what it sounds like," she said. "Private because the money wasn't raised in a public offering. Equity because it wasn't borrowed."

"It's a little too private for the Treasury Department's liking," Webster said. "The sources could be anyone from tax evaders to terrorists. The money could be invested to infiltrate any part of the economy. There is little information and even less control."

"What is Treasury looking for?"

"I think it goes back to the roots of the recession. No one paid attention to the hanky-panky in the home mortgage sector. The sub-prime market imploded and rippled into a financial crisis that destroyed more than a third of the world's wealth. In no time at all someone else's problem became Treasury's nightmare."

Flores remembered her last trip home. Even the secure suburban street where she grew up sprouted bank-owned for sale signs. She still dreaded calls from college friends wanting to meet for coffee or lunch. They would be hoping she knew of a full time career opening. She would feel guilty for a week after disappointing them.

"Private equity is a major player in more than one key industry," Webster said. "If there is pattern of exploitation developing, Treasury needs to know before more dominos start falling and the so-called new normal spins into global bankruptcy."

She wished she had paid more attention to what Bill told her he was working on. This was the first time her personal and professional lives had intersected. Service training seminars on the subject had gone in one ear and out the other. It was something she knew she could handle on her own. She was surprised at how queasy it made her feel.

"How did the Marshals Service get involved?"

"Earl Childers was a tier two player in private equity, one step below the decision makers. He knows how things work, as well as being privy to a number of recent and pending deals. Treasury wants him protected until they can get that information."

"Can't they interview him in a secure location?"

"There are no interviews," Webster said. "Childers spoke his piece at the trial and then clammed up. Same wall of silence Treasury has hit with everyone else in the industry."

She recalled how nervous Bill got whenever one of his work friends learned she was Federal heat. They weren't doing anything illegal. They just resented the Government on general principles. They resented any intrusion into their tight little circle. If Earl Childers' was an insider, his situation was probably thornier.

"Answering specific questions in court is one thing," she guessed. "Ratting out his entire business and social network is another."

"Childers' associates have shunned him since the trial," Webster said. "Ostracism is the normal witness retribution in white collar crime."

The Marshals Service couldn't prevent that. "What sort of threat are we supposed to protect him against?"

"Did you catch the San Francisco condominium fire on CNN?"

She recalled graphic film clips and dramatic narration as a backdrop to folding her laundry. Twelve people perished.

"So it wasn't an accident?" she asked.

"ATF says arson. They're still sorting out the chemistry. Point of origin was a unit where Childers was supposed to be attending a meeting."

"Doesn't that qualify him for witness protection?"

"Four people died in that unit. Childers would have made five. That means there was no better than a twenty percent chance he was targeted. And if he was, there is no evidence it was related to trial testimony."

"And your cronies don't think it was."

"My colleagues," Webster corrected, "think it unlikely that anyone capable of constructing a sophisticated firebomb would torch a twenty story building just to eliminate one man."

"Somebody must be worried about it."

An indulgent smile spread across Webster's face. "Treasury is just nervous."

"Why is the DC office handling a San Francisco assignment?"

"Treasury requested direct supervision by DC."

"And the Service is okay with that?"

"The command structure prefers to cement our image as team players rather than raise minor procedural issues."

Protect the empire. That was the message from the first day of Criminal Investigator Training Program/Basic Deputy US Marshal. The service had grown over two centuries from a scattering of district officials to an entrenched and powerful arm of the Justice Department, and the people in charge wanted to keep it that way.

She didn't bother to ask why she had been chosen for the assignment. In DC her suspension made her a potential drag on careers. A transfer might look like ethnic and gender bias. Routine surveillance wouldn't raise any eyebrows. In San Francisco, she would be out of sight, out of mind.

"The San Francisco Office will be expecting you," Webster went on. "Normal check-in procedure. Everything by the book."

She had just had her knuckles rapped. She probably shouldn't have saluted when she said, "Yes, Sir."

Webster leaned back and his chair squeaked under the weight. "Don't start developing an attitude, Tina. DC is a high visibility office."

Translation: she was a diversity hire and the Service was watching to see if there was any political mileage in moving her up the chain. Coming from Webster, it was intended as friendly advice from someone who had been there. She wondered if he had gotten so good at playing stereotype that he had come to believe his own fiction.

"Thanks, Web," was all she said.

She went back to her cube to boot up her computer. Her password had expired while she was on suspension. The Service was paranoid about computer security. Okay, maybe not paranoid. Low-lifes and crazies would have a field day if they could get into the system. She still resented having to execute the reset protocol and twiddle her thumbs through a virus scan.

Suspension had already given her too much time to think. She realized she was living the same stereotype as Howard Webster. She had allowed herself to be defined by her gender and her ethnicity. She was a woman. She should be a crusader, bent on shattering the glass ceiling. She was Latin. She should be a success, a role model for her culture. College had been a struggle, a time of triumphs and tears. Graduation had been a hard chair, a sore ass and three hours of boring speeches. She had won someone else's idea of victory, and it meant nothing to her.

The Marshals Service was more of the same. She had started in fugitive recovery. It wasn't slamming the door on one public menace after another that gave her satisfaction. It was the thrill of the chase that got her out of bed every morning, hungry for more. She was good. She was lucky. She wound up with the DC posting everyone coveted. Some posting. Errand girl. Schlepping prisoners and the occasional protection gig. She had no idea where her life was going, and she wasn't having any fun getting there. The sign-on screen popped up and brought her back to the problem at hand.

Earl Childers was a no-win assignment. The Treasury Department thought he was in danger. The Marshals Service thought Treasury was hyper-ventilating. If the Service was right, a good job would be just another day at the office. If Treasury was right, and situation went to hell, she would be blamed for screwing up a no-brainer. 24/7 coverage was out of the question. She would have to get inside Childers' head to anticipate the trouble he might get into.

A web search produced only a single item on Childers. He served on the Board of Directors of a firm called Hollister. Otherwise Treasury's would-be pigeon flew under the radar.

Hollister's web page advertised logistical services for the petroleum recovery industry. News items revealed the firm had been the subject of stock price manipulation. Two men were convicted. Probably the trial Childers testified in, although his name wasn't mentioned.

She decided against calling Bill Montgomery to see if he had heard of Childers. She didn't need another suspension. The first one still made her blood boil. She was going through the standard drill of chatting up a prisoner she had in transit. Normally it was a waste. Just a way to pass the miles. This one time she lucked into a domestic situation. The woman gave up the location of an outstanding fugitive. Flores felt the adrenaline she hadn't felt since she had been pulled out of the field and stuck in transport. The chase was on again, if only briefly and only by proxy. The location was a birthday party. The subject would be there only an hour or two. The Marshals Service had no resources close enough for a timely response. She called the FBI, who had obtained the arrest warrant.

Big mistake.

The nation's best-dressed law enforcement agency missed their man by five minutes. Rather than admit they took time to check their hair before they responded, they blamed her for delaying notification.

The Service was furious with her for calling the Bureau directly, violating referral procedures and crossing jurisdictional boundaries. Even her spotless six year record worked against her. She was experienced. She should have known better. No slack for trying to do the right thing and put a bad guy behind bars. Just thirty days of living on credit cards.

Okay. Fine. Finished business. She had a job to do. No B.S. this time. Stand up law enforcement duty. Twelve people dead and a Federal witness who could be number thirteen if she didn't get it right.

Chapter 3

*I*F HE WERE TO SET the scene to music, Philip Linfield would have selected *In the Hall of the Mountain King*. The stage was the atrium of a marble and glass skyscraper erected to serve notice that yet another Arab oil monarchy had stepped onto the world stage. The players were Bedouin elders accidentally come to wealth, men of tradition who lavished money on tailors to embellish the tribal robes of their meandering ancestors. They had come from the neighboring desert seeking parochial favors from their Prince. Linfield had journeyed halfway around the world to raise a billion dollars.

The Hollister acquisition and expansion was, by orders of magnitude, the most ambitious project he had undertaken to date. It would be his springboard to a position of influence, if not de facto control, in a major industrial segment.

An hour ago the Prince's thugs had met Linfield at the airport, ill-shaven wrestlers in silk suits and open collar shirts. They pre-empted Customs, turned out his pockets and searched his luggage. The ride through the city was an exercise in horn honking and light flashing, conducted without regard for law or safety. The sole exception was two blocks of respect and restraint while they passed a domed mosque attended by spiraling minarets. A reminder that Linfield was an infidel, alone and vulnerable in a land where Islam ruled supreme.

Their destination towered into an achingly bright sky. The few steps from passenger drop-off to the air-conditioned lobby raised perspiration inside Linfield's closely tailored shirt. The shirt was new, part of a business ensemble custom-made for this trip to project just the right combination of propriety and prosperity. He could only hope no stain would show at the collar.

A young woman swept his wardrobe with an admiring glance. She was tall, as sleek as an Arabian thoroughbred. Semitic features spoke of local origins, but eyeliner and lip gloss prepared him for a western education.

"Good morning, Mr. Linfield." Her voice was soft, her elocution flawless. "His Highness will see you shortly."

The fellow had a name, of course. One of those foot-long Arabic nightmares that traced his tribal ancestry and birthplace. To his entourage he was His Highness, or The Prince, as if there were only one and everyone should know who they were talking about.

"Please come this way," the woman said.

She led him along a concourse flanked by glittering shops. High heels tightened her calves and accentuated the smooth flow of her hips. While her business suit was conservative by western standards, here it was too risqué for street wear, and she would have to cover if she left the building. Linfield wondered if he was being tested, to see how he would behave in a foreign country, away from the prying eyes and wagging tongues of his own entourage.

The far end of the concourse was closed off by pocket doors, carved and inlaid in Saracen motif. A security guard was stationed there. He spread the doors only enough to pass Linfield and the woman. She stopped Linfield just inside.

"We will wait here," she said quietly and put a finger to her lips.

Linfield didn't take kindly to being shushed but instinct warned him to hold his tongue until he oriented himself.

The door closed and the noise of the concourse vanished into the hush of a two story atrium. Sunlight filtered through the smoked glass ceiling and illuminated intricate mosaics and finely woven tapestries. The Prince sat on a throne at the far end. Men were seated on embroidered pillows on the carpet before him, filling the atrium as they might once have filled a desert tent. Ceremonial stillness prevailed.

A name was called and one of the men rose. His beard was full and liberally salted with gray. He found his way forward among his peers at a pace that reflected age and infirmity as much as the solemn nature of the gathering and the personal pride he seemed to take in being allowed to participate.

The Prince rose for the ceremonial touching of cheeks. He sat down and his supplicant was bidden to sit at a low table that had the appearance of a slab of agate shaved flat and polished to a mirror sheen. Before the man was placed a plate of fruit, from which he took a single bite. It was inviolable custom in the Arab world that a host must provide refreshment for any guest, and that the guest may not refuse the offering. Once tradition had been honored, the man was permitted to speak. Linfield welcomed the opportunity to observe the routine, to get into harmony with the process.

Harmony was the key to any concert, fitting each individual performance into a synchronous whole. That was the spoken lesson from Linfield's father, who had hoped he would succumb to their shared love of music and seek a career as a symphony conductor.

The unspoken and more compelling lesson had come from watching too many times as his father put his own name before selection committees, only to be ignored in favor of those with gaudier pedigrees. Linfield instead applied his father's teachings to the free market of finance, where he answered neither to inept committees nor prying bureaucrats. His future was his own to create, his horizons limited only by his imagination, his willingness to embrace risk and his ability to comprehend and control the forces around him.

This would be Linfield's first, and perhaps only, face to face meeting with the one man who had displayed both the wealth and the willingness to fund the venture that would catapult him to global prominence and secure his position as a player in international finance.

"What is this event?" he asked the woman in a whisper.

"The council of tribal elders."

Linfield was still developing his fluency in Arabic; much of the dialect was beyond him. He asked his escort to translate.

She spoke in a barely audible voice, rendering exchanges into English as each elder was called forward. The upshot seemed to be that The Prince's blessing was required for everything from sewer contracts to marriages. Each petitioner withdrew an envelope from his robe and placed it reverently on the table. Probably the time honored way of funneling some of the ostensibly shared tribal wealth back to the royal coffers. The petitioner then stood and genuflected before he withdrew to make room for the next. Linfield was indeed in the Hall of the Mountain King.

His presence served no business purpose. Any last minute issues could be resolved via e-mail or Skype. Documents requiring signature could be exchanged by express courier. Funds would be transferred electronically. He had been summoned solely to demonstrate that he was at The Prince's beck and call. When his turn came, the woman led him forward, an immaculately groomed western trophy being paraded before the Prince's subjects.

This was the culmination of months of tedious negotiation with The Prince's functionaries. Linfield would have to play the simpering subordinate, if not to perfection, at least well enough to secure agreement from a fellow whose conceit had been bloated to monumental proportions by a lifetime of entitlement and privilege.

The Prince wore traditional garb, richly embroidered silk with a lordly headdress draped back over his right shoulder. He was heavy-set, unshaven as a show of Islamic piety, with soft jowls and a hooked nose. One cheekbone was slightly higher than the other, giving his face a warped and vaguely sinister cast. His eyes flashed with the adrenaline of a man reputed to love fast cars and faster women. Linfield pushed back the thought that a century ago the fellow would have been racing camels and copulating with girls who smelled of goat cheese rather than Chanel. He sat as he had seen the supplicants who preceded him sit.

Set before him was a bottle of Coca Cola in an ornate ice bucket. The Arab view of Americans. Soda guzzling imbeciles. Linfield took the required drink and smiled at his host.

The Prince spoke in Arabic solely for the benefit of his subjects. Linfield knew him to be a graduate of the London School of Economics, with superb English.

"Welcome, Mr. Linfield," his escort translated as a servant removed the bottle. "His Highness hopes that our climate is not too oppressive for you."

"Your Highness has mastered it completely," Linfield said, waving a hand at the glassed-in expanse of the air conditioned atrium. It wouldn't hurt to remind the fellow that his wealth and power rested on a foundation of western engineering.

"I was thinking beyond the climate," the Prince confided in English. "It might not go well with certain elements in your country or mine if the arrangement you propose becomes too public."

"Funds and ownership can be routed through intermediaries as required," Linfield assured him.

The Prince reverted to Arabic and the woman translated. "Sharia--the sacred law of Allah--forbids the payment or collection of interest."

That was more semantics than anything else. Money in Islamic countries was controlled by the chieftains and the church and when it was borrowed the amount would be greater than needed. The excess would go to the power structure in the form of graft or charitable donation. In the west, the tax authorities would quickly strip away the sham and declare the funds imputed interest. In the Middle East, the division was sacrosanct. The Prince had brought it up so he could cast himself as the defender of Islam before his followers.

"I am sure we can harmonize the returns from the project with Islamic Law," Linfield said.

The Prince went back to English. "Hollister's industrial control system," he said, and probed Linfield's eyes with his own, "remains state of the art?"

"Nothing in the world can match it," Linfield assured him. "It will become the standard for offshore drilling."

"Have there been any legal challenges to the ownership of the computer code?"

"None, Your Highness. The software was developed entirely within Hollister."

"And you are sure the firm can be taken private without attracting undue attention?"

"The shareholders have gone too long without dividends or increase in the market value of their shares. They will sell quickly and quietly at the right price, and as hungry as they are, that price should be reasonable."

A magnanimous smile lit The Prince's lopsided features. "Then let us move forward."

"Excellent, Your Highness."

The Prince's haughty demeanor returned. "The documents will be delivered to your Connecticut compound. My staff will be available to coordinate implementation of the agreements."

"Thank you, Your Highness, for sparing me your time."

Linfield had what he wanted. It was time to get out before this buffoon got completely carried away with his comic opera. Linfield stood, leaving his briefcase on the table.

The case was bought to be abandoned as a gift. It held a quarter of a million dollars in cash. A bribe, had The Prince been an official member of government. Since, despite all his posturing, the fellow was without portfolio and no better than fourteenth in line to rule his country, Linfield had booked the funds as reimbursement for analysis of the project, a position his lawyers could easily defend if the IRS ever stumbled on the entry.

The woman escorted Linfield out and deposited him in the lobby. His moment of glory was over. He was just another face in the crowd of westerners here to seek contracts and concessions.

Activity had shifted to the traffic circle in front of the building. Linfield watched the Prince's departure through tinted windows. The car was a stately old Rolls Royce, an outdated style called a landau, which had a convertible top that covered just the rear seat. The Prince had the top down, so his adoring subjects could get a parting look at him. Linfield smiled at the spectacle.

According to rumor, the Prince fancied himself a modern day Saladin, destined to lead his Muslim brethren to ultimate victory over the infidels. Linfield hoped the rumors were true. The larger the Prince's ego, the more money he could be cajoled into parting with to prove his importance. Linfield would have to move aggressively, though. There were undoubtedly others eager to exploit the fellow's weaknesses for their own gain.

The Prince's thugs appeared with Linfield's luggage, herded him out and installed him in the first in a line of waiting taxis for the trip to take him to the airport.

The teeming city raised another worry. Linfield needed to get The Prince's money transferred into a holding company account before some inconvenient revolution swept one more monarchy into the dustbin of history. Only then would the initial phase of his plan be complete.

The next phase would be more to his liking. With the Prince's money behind him, he could attack from a position of strength.

Chapter 4

*T*HE STARK CONFINES OF THE helicopter brought back visions of the Chinooks Earl Childers had ridden decades ago in Vietnam. This one was configured to carry drilling crews to an offshore oil platform. Hollister's officers and directors, a party of eighteen, were crammed shoulder to shoulder, strapped onto facing rows of canvas seats. Orange life jackets fastened over dress topcoats and high-end parkas made it clear they were out of their element. Facial expressions ranged from uncertain to stoic.

Only Philip Linfield was neither an officer nor a director. He had been introduced at the morning's formal board meeting as the source of the funding Hollister would need to exploit its newly developed technology. Linfield sat with Hollister's CEO. Sound deadening was nonexistent, and their conversation was swallowed by the slap-slap of idling rotor blades. Hydraulic pistons lifted the rear boarding ramp, dimming the interior of the machine. Turbines spun up and the helicopter rose into a buffeting wind. Childers closed his eyes and rolled with the turbulence.

Fatigue overtook him and Vietnam returned unbidden. He was a kid Lieutenant, less than a year after his commission from ROTC, looking out through the open doorway of a Huey helicopter at endless triple canopy jungle passing fifteen hundred feet below. Two streaks appeared just above the canopy. Ground attack jets. Wing tanks separated and napalm turned a small patch of green into an inferno. Helicopter gunships rolled in to rake the area with machine guns and rockets.

The Huey made a stomach-churning descent to treetop level. The air strike had fallen wide of its target and left the jungle intact to swallow them. Rotor blades barely cleared the nearest branches. Door gunners sprayed the trees, flailing at an enemy concealed in the dense vegetation. Childers and the assault troops could only hunker and wait to be hit by one of the incoming rounds popping through the fuselage.

Childers' eyes jerked open. Sweat was cold inside his shirt. The sight of familiar faces brought his heart rate down. The Chinook was descending. He turned his head to look out the porthole window behind him.

He had dozed off for some time. Their destination was visible below. A skeletal steel tower rose above a metal superstructure. Foam churned around massive hull columns and white-capped water stretched endlessly in every direction. Beneath the ocean lay millions of barrels of oil under intense pressure, a potential inferno that could dwarf all the napalm dropped in Vietnam. The sign visible when the Chinook bumped down on the helipad read *Welcome to Fort Apache*.

The rear ramp descended and cold air blew in, abating only a little when the rotors idled to a stop. Passengers unfastened their seat belts and came to their feet. Childers was slower than the rest; he could have been steadier.

The crew chief ushered them down the ramp double file. At the bottom each was handed a plastic hardhat. Childers' fit badly and sat high on his head. He had to hold it against the wind while he gripped a clammy metal handrail to maintain his balance.

"Mr. Childers, are you all right?"

The question came from Pilar Monterosa, Hollister's controller. A gust flattened her coat against slender curves and sent shoulder length hair whipping. A concerned smile clung to her lips. The attention was flattering, but emphasized that Childers was little more than a geriatric cancer survivor, a patient to be cared for.

"Fine, Pilar, thank you."

The insecurity in his legs made a liar of him. She stayed protectively close as they descended a flight of water-slickened metal stairs. The vibration of heavy machinery was a dull shudder underfoot. Wind whipped his visitor's badge into his face and twisted the strap around his neck.

The group filed into a windowless enclosure, careful not to disturb two men who sat at a table working keyboards and joysticks. Every eye was drawn to the wall in front of the operators, to a mosaic of flat screen monitors alive the with the flicker of colors and numbers, the jitter of bar charts, the spasmodic flow of sine waves. A steel door thunked against its weather stripping and closed out the noise of wind and machinery. Childers moved to the back where he could adjust his hard had without distracting from the proceedings.

"Ladies and gentlemen," Hollister's CEO said, "welcome to the next generation of industrial control systems."

The CEO was Dylan Quist, a ruddy and slightly plump man just short of fifty who compensated for average stature by attacking even the simplest tasks with an overblown show of energy. His Harvard MBA, a spotty resume and a boundless ego had made him the only viable candidate willing to replace the man whose missteps put Hollister on the verge of bankruptcy four years ago.

Quist's audience listened dutifully through his spiel about reduced labor costs, enhanced efficiency and greater safety. The accomplishments were the work of two software engineers. The pair had made considerable money early in their careers and committed part of their fortunes to buy into Hollister when it was desperate for cash. The stolid Hendrick took over an unattended workstation to demonstrate the computer system that controlled the platform. Nisham, the upper-caste Indian, addressed the group in flawless Imperial English.

"We came with a shared vision," he began. "Partnering with the firm afforded us the opportunity to realize our dream and elevate the standards of capability and profitability for robotic control applications."

After years of setbacks and struggles, a prototype was finally installed on a working platform. Childers allowed himself a sense of pride.

Nisham covered everything from the constantly varying load on the massive generators that fed electricity through the copper arteries of the platform to pressures in the piping to the status of fire-fighting and emergency shutdown systems.

He concluded with, "may I answer any questions?"

"My granddaughter," one woman piped up, "had her facebook account hacked. Can that happen here?"

Should control of the platform fall into the wrong hands, the results could be catastrophic. Beyond fire and loss of life, there was the potential for an uncontainable oil spill in the millions of gallons riding currents and tides toward the California coast.

"The platform is not run on a server that might be attacked through a robotic network," Nisham said. "We employ a device called a programmable logic controller. It would require physical access to the hardware and intimate knowledge of the redundant firewalls for even the most skilled hacker to embed malicious code."

The pair received polite applause. Their investment had been the angel capital that took the project from concept to reality. Childers knew that making it commercially viable would require a vastly greater investment in marketing, production and installation.

The kind of money only a firm like Linfield's could broker. It was surprising that Linfield hadn't brought engineers to watch the demonstration; that a senior financial executive would trust two men just barely thirty who wore parkas with last season's ski lift tags still attached. The fact that he hadn't delegated the project to one of his subordinate managers suggested it was unusually important to him. Childers moved close to Pilar.

"Any information on the mount of Mr. Linfield's capital infusion?"

"It's not been shared," she said. "At least not down to my level."

"It will soon. You're in charge of accounting."

"I shouldn't be able to divulge specifics unless all board members are notified," she reminded him.

Childers had noted on past occasions that she had an odd and probably unconscious habit of slipping into British phrasing when she was nervous. She either knew or expected more than had been disclosed in the Board meeting. Questions would only alienate her.

"If you hear anything in a general way," Childers said, "would you please let me know?"

She gave him a reassuring smile.

Her closeness and fragrance were stirring. It was too late in life for foolishness. Childers stepped back to maintain his dignity, pretending to listen to the remainder of Quist's prepared remarks.

The Platform master took over for a tour of the facility. It was a trip across slippery, pierced-steel planking, made miserable by wind chill and blowing salt spray. The crew members they encountered were robust men dressed in heavy boots, water-repellent coats, mufflers, and caps with earflaps under their hard hats. Men comfortable with heavy machinery and willing to endure two week shifts under primitive conditions for the money and bragging rights that went with them. They were absorbed in work and seemed oblivious to the parade of strangers winding its way through their domain.

The Platform Master stopped the group to explain the workings of the motion compensator that offset the rig's movement in the sea to keep the drill bit stationary in the hole. The subject was dull and the group paid scant attention, distracted by the arrival of a supply boat.

The platform was a self-contained community, with ongoing needs and limited storage. Constant replenishment was essential. The supply boat, a service provided by Hollister, was the isolated structure's lifeline. Docking in heavy seas was a perilous ballet, intricate enough to require the boat's entire deck crew as well as men on the platform. The Master gave up on his lecture and led the group toward a railing where they could look down for a better view. Childers found his way blocked by Philip Linfield.

Linfield waited until they were alone before he spoke. "Do you know who I am?"

His voice and manner were polished and patrician, and left no doubt that there was more to know than his introduction had provided.

"Your firm is widely known," was all Childers had to offer. Few details about Linfield's transactions ever reached the public domain.

"We need to talk," Linfield said.

"Go ahead."

"Privately," Linfield said.

Childers didn't like being singled out for special attention. Decades of negotiating experience warned him it was a tactical error to let his counter-party set the time, place and agenda. It might, however, be an opportunity to learn why a man of Linfield's stature had come in person to this far reach of civilization.

"At your convenience, then," Childers conceded.

"I'll have my staff set something up." Linfield started away to rejoin the group, but turned. "Oh, and Childers, no one of any consequence wears button-down collars."

Linfield was gone, but his remark lingered. Childers had worn button-down collars since college, even going as far as to have shirts custom-made when they were not in fashion. They were a connection to his debut in the world beyond the small town where he grew up. For so light a subject to draw comment from a man of Linfield's sophistication raised questions about what might be percolating behind his suave exterior.

The tour resumed as soon as the supply boat was secure. The wind was gaining intensity, drawing clouds up out of the distance like the foothills of a gathering storm. There were no complaints when the time came to board the helicopter for the ride back.

The last few days had seen Childers move from his hotel to his new home in the suburbs. He was far from settled. The simplest unpacking chores wore him out, forcing him to pace himself, frustrated that his stamina no longer seemed equal to his plans. Now it seemed Hollister might demand a greater share of his limited energy. The obvious solution was to walk away. Resign his position on the board. Sell his stock. Put the whole episode behind him and get on with the quiet retirement he had earned.

The sense of duty that nagged him to stay on and finish the turnaround he had helped initiate could be dismissed as ego. He was no longer an important cog in the machinery that kept the company moving forward.

What he couldn't shake was the forty years of survival instinct that had infiltrated and gradually co-opted his thinking, the visceral certainty that as soon as he turned his back someone would find a way to stick a knife in it.

Chapter 5

*J*UST THE IDEA OF AN interagency meeting was enough to set Valentina Flores' nerves on edge. Particularly here in San Francisco, where she knew none of the players. A last minute call from the local Marshals' office and an unfamiliar downtown building address conspired to make her late. She had no chance to compose herself before the receptionist paged the conference room.

The woman who stepped out might have been as young as her late forties. Between Clairol and Botox it was hard to tell anymore. Her hair was a salon wave, her suit smartly tailored. Three inch pumps brought her up to Flores' five feet nine.

"Alexis Tremaine," she said. "Supervising Special Agent, FBI Field Office. Come in, please."

Flores had guessed FBI from the outfit but she hadn't expected the highest ranking agent in the city. She regretted her decision that a no-contact surveillance would allow jeans, flat heels and a pony tail. All she could do was hide her misgivings behind a smile.

The conference room was furnished to accommodate ten but only two men sat at the table. The younger was an Asian-American. Pinstripes weren't enough to pass him off as an investment banker. On Wall Street they knew how to tie a Windsor knot. Men from Washington always wound up with a lopsided mess and an embarrassing dimple.

"Roland Ohashi, Treasury," the man said. "You are the Marshal in charge of the Earl Childers detail?"

"Valentina Flores."

She saw no point in mentioning that she was the detail, or that Treasury's instructions to have no contact with Childers had forced her to leave him alone on a helicopter on its way to an offshore oil platform.

Ohashi's companion was a middle-aged man who managed a rumpled look in spite of an expensive suit. His tousled hair was thinning on top, his smile a disarming display of smoker's teeth.

"Levi Weiss," he said. "Attorney General's Office. Earl Childers was my witness in Manhattan. And yes, you may sit down."

Flores waited until Tremaine seated herself. The woman had a dancer's flexibility and a lot of practice in tight skirts. Flores sat next to her, across from the two men.

"Sorry I'm late," she said. "Short notice. Could someone please tell me what the meeting is about?"

"The subject," Ohashi said with a withering look at Tremaine, "is Earl Childers. A man for whom we arranged protection and to whom we expected to have exclusive access. I fly out from DC to arrange a critical interview and I find the FBI planning to interrogate him."

Tremaine just smiled. "How much were you told about the fire at the Savannah Condominium Tower?"

"ATF is investigating it as arson," Ohashi said.

"Some of the bomb components were of foreign military origin," Tremaine said. "The fire has been classified as a terrorist act. The investigation has been placed in FBI jurisdiction."

Flores' heart sank. She was in the middle of another interagency spat. It was time to lower her profile. Listen politely. Smile a lot. Don't get involved.

"Childers has information regarding a potential acquisition in a key industrial sector," Ohashi said.

"Childers was invited to a meeting at the time and place of the bombing," Tremaine said. "That raises any number of possibilities. We would be derelict if we failed to examine them."

"We need answers from Childers," Ohashi insisted. "We may not get them if he is antagonized by a misdirected criminal investigation."

"We are going to interview Childers," Tremaine said. "I was instructed to notify Treasury as a courtesy."

"I want the interview delayed for a day or two at least. I need time to talk to my people in DC to find out what they want to do."

"Marshal Flores," Tremaine said, "the Service has designated you as their representative in this matter. Do you have any concerns that questioning Childers might compromise your assignment?"

Flores needed a politically correct answer. "Close of business in DC is 2:00 PM here. I'll do my best to have a response by then."

"Has your surveillance raised any concerns?"

Another no-win question. Any opinion she ventured could come back to haunt her. Best to stick to the facts.

"Childers moved out of his hotel the morning I arrived and moved into his new home south of the city. He's spent the last couple of days at home, probably unpacking."

Flores held her breath, wondering if Tremaine would ask for his current location and coverage.

"How secure is his residence?"

"It's a large house in an open neighborhood. Surrounded by a hedge and eight foot wrought iron fencing. Gated driveway. I ran the neighbors through NCIC, no criminal backgrounds."

Ohashi nodded agreement. "They're all software types from Silicon Valley. The house is based on a Frank Lloyd Wright original somewhere in the Midwest. Built for a little over four million. Childers bought it out of foreclosure for just less than three."

Flores had guessed the property was expensive but the actual numbers were head-spinning. Her parents had struggled for thirty years to pay off a mortgage that wasn't a tenth of that size.

Tremaine compressed her lips, irritated by the interruption. "Mr. Weiss, does the Attorney General's Office have any concerns regarding the Childers interview?"

The trial was last month's news, and Flores was alert for any clue why Weiss was still involved.

"I'll have to put the question to my people and get back to you," he told Tremaine. "Just as a heads-up, they'll probably lobby to have me at the table."

Tremaine took her smart phone out of a waist clip and checked her schedule. "We will meet again day after tomorrow to finalize the interview protocol."

Tremaine set a time, entered it on her calendar and replaced the phone.

"I'll need to excuse myself now," and as an aside to Flores, added, "hopefully this taxi driver will be a little more civil than the last."

Flores knew a cue when she heard one. As supervising agent, Tremaine controlled the FBI motor pool in the city. She would need a ride only when it suited her purposes.

"I can drop you," she said. "I'm parked in the basement garage."

Childers wouldn't be back for at least an hour. Spending time trapped in a car with a senior FBI official wouldn't be fun, but Flores might be able to use the opportunity to get some insight into the situation she'd been thrown into. And she might as well stick her neck out and try to build some rapport.

"Ballroom or ballet?" Flores asked as the two women rode down in the elevator.

"Excuse me?"

"Dance training is easy to spot," Flores said. "I taught Latin American to make up the difference between my student loan and the actual cost of college."

"Tango," Tremaine said. "I caught the bug from my former husband."

Her tone was reserved enough to close the subject. Flores couldn't tell whether her reticence was personal or just a supervisor maintaining appropriate detachment. They crossed the garage to Flores' sedan in silence.

"What did you think of Childers' profile," Tremaine asked when they were out on the street and underway.

"I didn't know there was one."

FBI profiles took time to develop. If they had one on Childers, then he had been a person of interest before the Savannah firebombing.

"Anything in the contents that might help me get inside his head?" Flores asked.

"He's an odd duck," Tremaine said. "A kid from east nowhere who grew up to play big league finance. The few people who remembered him from college gave vague descriptions of a business school nerd. Commissioned into the Army during the Vietnam build-up. MBA on the GI Bill following his discharge. Nothing to distinguish him from thousands of other young men on the same track. People who worked with him over the years characterized him as a head-down, get-it-done type.

"Last year he was diagnosed with cancer. The surgery was successful but complications left him at death's doorstep. He's spent most of the time since recovering. Treasury is hoping the experience will cause him to re-evaluate his life and decide to answer their questions. The profiler said they might as well interview the Easter Bunny. Childers is an isolated soul who adjusts only as much as his surroundings require."

There were times when Flores could cast herself in the same role, an outsider trying to fit into an alien social structure, burying herself in work because that was where her intuition and initiative might count for something. She stopped in front of the Federal Building and wondered why the meeting hadn't been held here.

Tremaine would have a private office and her position would give her priority on conference rooms. For some reason the meeting had been kept off the record and under wraps. Tremaine thanked her for the ride and vanished into the building.

The FBI profile on Childers was a clever way to communicate significant interest in him without saying specifically what the interest was. Tremaine had shared only benign details, but in a way that underscored that Childers was FBI, not Treasury, property. If agencies were choosing sides for a jurisdictional squabble, Flores needed back-up. She got the car underway and called Howard Webster on her cell phone to bring him up to speed.

"I'll run it up the food chain to be sure," Webster said, "but you'd better plan on observing the interview. If we pass up the opportunity, it will look like we don't have our heads in the game."

"Okay. Thanks, Web."

He volunteered no further information about Childers and she saw no point in asking. This was one of a shitload of assignments he was monitoring. Childers was just another computer file for him to keep up to date. Flores was responsible for the field work, and no one had her back.

Until this morning she had seen Childers as nothing more than a self-indulgent old man with too much money. Now she needed to know what made him important and what made him tick. She parked under a dismal overcast near where Childers' helicopter would land and used her cell phone again.

"Bill Montgomery."

The soft purr of his voice sent a shiver up her spine. "Drop your calculator. Come out with your hands up."

"Hey, Wyatt Earp. I thought you were on the west coast."

"I could wiggle my toes in the Pacific Ocean."

"So this isn't social."

Only in her dreams. "Do you know a man named Earl Childers?"

"I know the name." A hint of caution in his voice.

"This isn't interrogation," she said.

"What, then? Secret mission? Double Oh Seven?"

"Licensed to thrill," she said. "Seriously, anything you've heard about him."

"Testified in a trial in New York."

"And been a pariah ever since?"

"Tina, we're not the Mafia. It's just that having a Federal witness in the room stifles discussion."

That explained why the finance industry was nervous about Childers, but not what he might be up to now that had several branches of government interested in him.

"Ever hear of a company named Hollister?"

"A lot of whispers. Something big is about to break. I can ask around. Try to get some specifics."

"No, that's okay."

"No, my pleasure. There may be an opportunity in this. Look, I'll have to get back to you."

"No, Bill, seriously--"

He was gone and she was left with the fear that he would blunder into some official's career-building inquiry. She had heard her share of horror stories. People on the fringes of some activity, with no criminal knowledge or intent, who were strong-armed into pleading out on a technicality to justify the cost of a failed investigation.

Redial got his voicemail. Shit. The flashing beacon of the Chinook was visible beneath the clouds, coming in fast.

Chapter 6

PHILIP LINFIELD FOLLOWED THE MAITRE'D among dim lit tables, with a critical ear cocked toward the pianist. The piece was the R&B standard *Since I Met You Baby,* played in the richness of full verse rather than just the melody line over chords favored by most commercial performers. The nuances of top line fingering might have been more subtle, but overall it was a satisfactory rendering, suitable to the venue.

Dylan Quist had touted Falcon's Roost as San Francisco's most exclusive restaurant. It occupied an upper floor in a premier high-rise tower and offered a spectacular view, with just hint of fog drifting in the distant lights of the Golden Gate Bridge. The patrons were an eclectic mix of business people and couples. This was a place of grand aspirations for both the boardroom and the bedroom.

Dinner was at Quist's invitation. The poor fellow probably saw it as an opportunity to unveil some delusional vision for Hollister. The reservation proved to be a window table for two. Having the city spread beneath him might inflate Quist's ego, but the quiet atmosphere would militate against any untoward outburst arising from his inevitable disappointment.

Quist stood with an effusive greeting and his usual overbearing handclasp. Somewhere the fellow had found a competent tailor. A well-dressed huckster was still a huckster, but at least it wouldn't be an embarrassment to be seen with him. Linfield allowed the Maitre'd to seat him.

Quist established himself in his chair and spoke in an ecstatic hush. "I'm glad you could make it out for today's demonstration, Philip."

Linfield remained silent. Best to let the fellow to exhaust his enthusiasm before they got down to cases.

"I trust you agree with me," Quist went on, "that Hollister's advances in technology position the firm to claim a significant share of the industrial control systems market in offshore oil recovery."

Linfield took his napkin from its silver ring and spread it carefully on his lap. "I wouldn't have undertaken the trip myself if I had any doubts."

"Then this might be a good time to discuss the specifics of funding," Quist suggested.

"I'm sorry. Funding?"

"The money to bring the new technology to market." Quist's smile flickered when Linfield showed no response. "Just a handshake on the general terms," he added quickly.

"That's quite unnecessary," Linfield said.

"I don't understand?"

"It couldn't be simpler. Hollister will be become the private subsidiary of a Swiss holding company. Expansion will be directed and funded by the parent firm."

The server arrived with breadsticks and menus and began rattling off the specials. It was a welcome opportunity for Linfield to compose himself. The next few minutes would be critical. Any objections Quist might raise had to be quashed to expedite the acquisition.

Mounting panic in Quist's eyes made it clear that the full import of Linfield's declaration was dawning on him.

"Philip," he said as soon as the server was out of earshot, "my request was for expansion funding, not a buyout of the firm."

"I don't recall any restrictions on how the funding was to be structured."

"I was thinking in terms of a cash infusion in return for an equity interest."

"Then you should have said so, Dylan."

"Philip, you can't just take a publicly traded company private."

"Why not?"

"Certainly not without consulting me. After all, I am Chairman of Hollister's Board. I do have directors who will need to sign off."

"Simply tell them that their shares will be bought at current market value," Linfield said.

"Current market value?"

Linfield ignored Quist's incredulous stare. Best to give the fellow a little more time to adapt to his new situation. Linfield opened his menu and perused the selections.

"What do you recommend, Dylan? I seldom get out to sample west coast fare. I was hoping for Copper River Salmon, but I don't see it here."

"The Copper River run is short. Only a few weeks."

"Too bad," Linfield said, and went on studying his options.

"Philip," Quist said, "you are as aware as I am that the current stock price is artificially low. Wall Street is still wondering if we can raise the capital to exploit our product advantages. They won't bid up the price until they are sure."

"You can hardly blame them," Linfield said. "Marketing will be costly. You will have to buy complex hardware and pay premium wages for specialized labor to install it under primitive and perilous conditions, all before you see a nickel of return. Do you have the capital to finance that sort of undertaking?"

"That's why I contacted your firm."

"Then you must agree that any increase in share price is the result of the infusion of capital, and that increase should accrue to those who infuse the capital."

Linfield closed his menu. He had set the music on the rack. Quist would have to render his best solo.

"The force behind this is the end of the offshore drilling moratorium," Quist argued. "New platforms will incorporate new technology. Older facilities will need to upgrade to compete."

The fellow was simply parroting the scribbling of public analysts.

"Dylan, there is no time for nonsense. Your competitors are not standing still. The Germans, the Japanese, the others can field upgraded systems in a year, no more than two. Unless you have a solid installed base before then, your window of opportunity will have closed. It's like the Copper River Salmon. Eat while they are running or you don't eat at all."

Indignation made a thermometer of Quist's face. "None of this would be possible if I hadn't built Hollister to where it is today."

"If you hadn't built Hollister?" Linfield asked.

"Yes."

"Dylan, if any single man is responsible for Hollister's current position, it would be Earl Childers. Is he not the one who introduced the two gentlemen whose investment bailed the firm out of impending bankruptcy and who developed the technology?"

Indirectly it was Childers who brought Hollister to Linfield's attention. The fellow had filed a criminal complaint with the Department of Justice. Newspaper coverage of the resulting trial had alerted Linfield to Hollister's potential.

According to reliable industry gossip a deal had gone wrong and Childers was left to take the blame. He had apparently been up to the challenge, finding two software engineers with money and motivation whose work positioned the company for international leadership. Quist had been recruited by the Board simply to provide business management.

A cocktail waitress arrived and Linfield ordered a Manhattan. Quist did likewise, possibly an effort to pretend he was on equal footing.

"Childers is still on the Board," Quist pointed out. "He may have something to say about this."

The fact that Childers had gone to the Justice Department was troubling. He was experienced enough to know that the finance industry would never let a good deed go unpunished. Anyone convicted at trial would be back in business within a year of leaving prison. Once Childers testified, he would never work another deal as long as he lived. Linfield could only guess what he had been thinking.

At best the fellow's behavior would be unpredictable. His financial stake in Hollister could conceivably provide misplaced incentive to resist a buyout. That made it imperative to remove him from the mix. The separation would have to be done adroitly, so as not to attract any unwanted attention.

"You leave Earl Childers to me," Linfield told Quist. "He is too much for you to handle."

"Philip, I don't want to start a fight over this."

"A fight?" Linfield asked, letting amusement filter into his voice.

Quist forced a conciliatory smile. "There must some middle ground. Something we can work out, if we put our minds to it."

There was no point telling the fellow that commitments had been made. It would only raise questions that were better left unasked.

"I need a proposal I can take to the board," Quist said. "Something I can recommend in good conscience."

The server arrived and asked if they were ready to order. Swordfish seemed appropriate for the occasion. Quist ordered New York steak, perhaps a feeble declaration of independence. There was nothing to be gained by further sparring. It was time to go for the jugular.

"Look here, Dylan, you have no ground to stand on. Your two largest stockholders need cash. Their investment in Hollister has yet to produce a return, the recession has eroded their fortunes and there is at least one potentially litigious divorce in the offing. They will sell because they have to and the others will follow their lead because the company and its stock price would collapse without them."

"Well, you've done your homework," Quist conceded.

Linfield tasted his Manhattan cocktail. It was like a lot of things on the West Coast, passable but lacking that indefinable touch of culture. He managed a smile for Quist.

"Dylan, we are about to embark on an exciting adventure, and we'd like to have you along. Your leadership over the last four years has been valuable. You will continue as CEO under contract. There will be bonus opportunities."

Quist stared morosely out the window at the gathering dusk.

"Of course," Linfield said, "if you have other opportunities you prefer to pursue, naturally we will respect your wishes."

Quist's head snapped around. "I see now where the term 'pirate equity' came from."

"Dylan, I would like to enjoy my meal. I won't be able to do that if you are going to spend the evening moping."

Quist fell silent.

Linfield wondered if the fellow had grasped that his days with Hollister were numbered. He had been naïve enough to expect that Linfield would be content with fees and perhaps a minority stock position. He seemed ignorant of the international leverage Hollister might realize under proper guidance.

Beyond Linfield's own ambitions, there was the country to consider. Too much American leadership had been squandered by short-sighted management and fractious government. It was time to reverse the trend. If that required middle-eastern money and a façade of European holding companies, so be it.

It wouldn't happen the way it was taught in business school. Current players in the industry wouldn't surrender market share without a fight, and in their view anything worth fighting for was worth fighting dirty for. That meant spurious lawsuits, political influence and whatever chicanery the situation allowed. The Hollister response would have to meet any challenge without exceeding the bounds of propriety.

Quist lacked both the nerve and the polish to participate at that level. His only value was transitional stewardship until a more seasoned team could be put in place. If the fellow's ego didn't allow him to see that, there could be some unpleasantness.

Chapter 7

EARL CHILDERS TIMED THE PHONE call for just after nine AM. It would be noon in Manhattan. Restaurants would be filling with executives making too much of things they could have settled in an e-mail exchange.

"Ray Parker."

"Earl Childers, Ray. The big boys left you out of their lunch plans again?"

"Christ, Earl, are you trying to get me fired?"

"So I'm still the industry leper?"

"What were you thinking, going to the US Attorney?"

"The business doesn't need criminals, Ray."

"Yeah, but the two guys who hung you out to dry on the Hollister deal. That makes it look personal."

Four years ago it was personal. Two private equity partners had accumulated a block of Hollister stock and offered Childers an ownership interest to represent them on the board of directors. Rumors of an impending loan to fund the firm's growth drove the stock price up. The two partners sold at a tidy profit. The loan never materialized. Share value plummeted. The situation smelled of fraud and Childers went to the US Attorney.

He was surprised when he was summoned to testify at trial three years later. Fraud cases were almost always settled out of court with a money fine. This time the government assigned a prosecutor and litigated to conviction.

"Water over the dam," was all he said to Parker. "What is the street talk on Spencer Van Wyck?"

"He got fricasseed. Don't you get CNN on your side of the country?"

"What was Van Wyck doing in San Francisco?"

"How would I know?" Parker asked. "I'm just the jerk nobody invites to lunch."

"See if you can find out, will you?"

"What kind of attention will I be drawing?"

"In an industry full of ghouls? You'll draw attention if you're not curious."

"Come on, Earl, Van Wyck was from the social stratosphere. Why do you care what he was doing?"

"He invited me to a meeting. I would have been caught in the fire if I had gone."

Parker was silent for a moment. "Why would Van Wyck ask you to a meeting?"

The question had dogged Childers for days. News reports told him little. The people who died in the unit with Van Wyck were a class action lawyer, a reformed computer hacker and an associate professor of engineering. Childers knew none of them.

"Just ask around, will you Ray?"

"Look, Earl, I know I owe you because I was included in a couple of big paydays, but there is a limit to how far my neck goes out."

"I'd also appreciate anything you can find out about Hollister," he said. "I think it may be in play."

It had taken years to bring the firm back from the brink of ruin. He questioned whether he could muster the will or the stamina to go through it again, and flinched at the thought of what Parker might turn up.

"Do what I can," was Parker's grudging promise. "Just don't call me here again. Okay?"

"Thanks, Ray."

Childers hung up. He had never been comfortable calling in favors, but now he was isolated and he saw no choice. Until he heard back from Parker, there was nothing he could do but get on with his new life.

GPS directions took him to a building in a light industrial suburb. The sign read *Concorso d'Italia.* From inside came the intermittent snarl of a high-performance engine. Childers found his way in through a cluttered little office.

The building was organized into maintenance bays holding automobiles in various stages of disassembly. Tools were hung with obsessive symmetry and the concrete floor was clean enough to eat off. Two men in coveralls hunched over the open hood of a coupe, working the controls and listening to the result. Childers went over.

"Excuse me," he said. "I'm looking for Pietro Sambatero."

The shorter of the two men stepped away from the car. He was broad and swarthy, with the sharp eyes and ready smile of a man accustomed to dealing.

"I am Pietro," he said over the burble of the idling engine.

"My name is Earl Childers, Mr. Sambatero. I was given your name as the best classic Ferrari source in the area."

Sambatero patted the coupe he was working on. "Do you know what this is?"

The question tested Childers' tact as well as his knowledge. "I'm not looking for a Maserati. Even an A6G as nice as this one."

"One of only twenty-one from the Allemano coachworks," Sambatero said. "It will be consigned for auction next month, if it is not sold first."

"It wouldn't cross the block for less than seven figures," Childers said. "That's too much money to put on the road."

Childers had spent part of his convalescence reading up on the Italian sports car market. He knew he would have to talk a good game make a deal.

"What are you looking for?"

"A 250 GTE."

Sambatero led him out to a satellite building that held ragged rows of cars awaiting attention. Accumulated filth masked the color of a low coupe but the shape was unmistakable. Childers had first seen it when he went to college; a source of awe and envy to a small town freshman, lost and alone in a crowd of thousands, all more socially and financially secure than he.

"Not in the best condition," Sambatero said, pulling open the driver's door to gauge Childers' reaction.

It didn't matter that the upholstery was coming loose at the seams, the dashboard paint was chipped and the instrument bezels were tarnished. The sight filled him with dread that he might never find another.

"How much?" he asked. "Road worthy. Fresh paint and interior."

"The car I can sell for a hundred thousand as is. Restoration is labor and materials. I can do an estimate, but it won't be cheap. The engine needs a full re-build. Twelve cylinder Columbo, it won't be cheap."

It was ridiculous money for a juvenile fantasy, but this was a relic of his days as a four-eyed nobody; wearing his toy soldier suit on Fridays because ROTC wasn't an option when your old man had been wounded at Anzio and studying on weekends because there was no money for anything else.

"Will you need a deposit?"

"Not for the estimate. Car will be cash before any work starts. We will have to agree payments and timing for restoration."

Childers left his contact information and drove to a rifle range. He paid for a lane and targets and took the Winchester to a shooting station. The recoil from the first round wasn't the jolt he recalled from his boyhood. His Army marksmanship training had stayed with him. The range telescope showed a hole in the black. Repeat shots generated a group just over three inches at one hundred yards. Luck was certainly a factor. No vintage rifle was that precise, he hadn't shot any firearm in decades and at his age he was looking at the world through progressive lenses. Fatigue was creeping into his bones and he left without shooting the rest of his ammunition, content with a few minutes of vicarious youth.

Lunch and a nap gave Childers the energy to face another afternoon of settling into his new home. The house was larger than any place he had ever lived, its size justified only because the cavernous interior offered enough room for the furnishings he had acquired to create his vision of a retirement sanctuary, and enough built-in shelving to properly organize his lifetime hoard of books and magazines. The phone interrupted just before five. He was glad of a chance to sit where he could warm himself in the brief burst of late sun slanting through clerestory windows set just below the eight foot ceilings.

"Ray Parker, Earl. You alone?"

"Is it that serious?"

"You could be up to your ass in alligators."

"Spare me the clichés."

"Okay, the first tidbit comes from the grapevine. According to what Van Wyck's wife has been dishing to the high society sisterhood, hubby comes back from a business trip to the Middle East white as a sheet. He goes to his bosses at the bank about whatever it is, and they blow him off. Next, she says he's looking for anyone in authority at Hollister. Somebody reminds him you are on the Board and he's on the first thing flying for the West Coast. Two days later, he's a crispy critter."

"Hollister is strictly domestic," Childers said. "No foreign operations. Certainly not in the Middle East."

"You asked what I heard. That's what I heard."

"Any idea what he wanted to see me about?" Childers asked.

"That's what nobody can figure. Van Wyck is Ivy League. He wouldn't know how to rock the boat if he wanted to. You, on the other hand, are small time, big trouble. No offense, Earl."

"None taken. What's the next tidbit?"

"Before the day is out, I get a call from a reporter for the *Wall Street Journal*. Wants to meet for cocktails."

"I'm impressed," Childers said. "The *Journal* never gave me anything but a chump discount on my subscription renewal."

"They are very interested in whatever it was Van Wyck got onto the in Middle East."

"Do they have any clue?"

"No. But apparently the investigation into the fire that killed Van Wyck and the others has been bucked up to the FBI. If I were you, Earl, I'd find a criminal attorney who knows how the Bureau works."

"Am I suspected of something?"

"I don't know, but if the *Journal* has their teeth into this, it's not good news. Like one step below *Sixty Minutes'* cameras showing up at the office."

"Sorry, Ray. I didn't mean to drag you into anything."

"Little late for that, Earl. This broad thinks she's onto something, and she's not going away."

"What are you hearing about Hollister?"

"Noise on the street. Something big brewing. Philip Linfield's name came up."

"I know that much," Childers said.

"Then you know I won't hear shit. Linfield's not New York. He runs his operation from a mink-lined concentration camp in Connecticut. A lot of information goes in there. None ever comes out."

"Linfield is in San Francisco," Childers said.

"The man himself?"

"Yes, but he's not doing the kind of diligence that goes with a major investment."

"That means he has someone inside Hollister," Parker said. "Feeding him what he needs to know."

"Can you ask the girl friend if she knows who it is?"

"How would she know?"

"The *Journal* is interested in Van Wyck. Van Wyck was interested in Hollister."

"You ask her. She's bound to call you."

"You know I can't talk to her, Ray. I'm on Hollister's Board. That puts me under a non-disclosure agreement."

"So Ray 'The Patsy' Parker is out front again?"

"Spare me the drama. She's only a reporter."

"Just remembering what I learned from a guy named Earl Childers. Trust no one. Only the paranoid survive."

"Thanks, Ray. Let me know what you hear."

Childers ended the call.

Parker had just written his epitaph. If he was remembered at all it would be as one more financial operative, paranoid about being conned and vindictive when it happened. No expensive toys and no amount of daydreaming would turn back the calendar to an innocent youth. It was time to focus on the situation confronting him now.

The Savannah firebombing was connected with Hollister, but apparently not with Childers' trial testimony. The connection had something to do with a banker's trip to the Middle East, where Hollister had no presence. It had claimed the lives of a group of people Childers had never heard of. None of it seemed to make sense.

A private equity player named Philip Linfield had Hollister in his sights. A connection there seemed unlikely. Coercion was common enough in finance, but the arm-twisting was always verbal. Violence was unheard of. Whatever Van Wyck had discovered about Hollister was more sinister than the usual scheming that went along with profit and loss.

Linfield's behavior remained unexplained. He had left his financial empire in the hands of subordinates and come in person to the West Coast. His agenda must go beyond a simple investment in Hollister. How far and in what direction Childers might learn soon. Linfield's representative had called to arrange a face to face meeting.

Until he understood the situation and the specific threat, Childers couldn't guarantee his own safety by simply selling his Hollister shares on the open market and walking away. There was nothing to do but call the security company to make sure the house alarm was properly activated.

Chapter 8

ALENTINA FLORES MADE SURE SHE arrived early for the meeting to coordinate Childers' FBI interview. Killing time in the building lobby, she found an e-mail from Bill on her cell phone. No call. Not even a text. Just a mail from his corporate account. She had a mental picture of him in his cube, ticker screens flashing in front of him, talking on his headset while he typed: *Hey, Wyatt. Hollister definitely in play. Leapfrog technology. Top tier broker. Major money. Stay tuned. Junior G-Man signing off.* Well, at least she was still on her guy's radar. She caught an elevator up to the FBI offices.

Handling the Childers surveillance by herself left no time for a salon appointment, so she couldn't do anything about the pony tail. Wardrobe was another story. Straight skirt and business jacket. Three inch heels brought her height to a full six feet. If she was going to be Wyatt Earp, she might as well look the part.

Levi Weiss and Roland Ohashi were seated in the reception area. Weiss smiled, relaxed and rumpled. Ohashi gave her a curt nod, visibly tense in freshly pressed pinstripes, with one leg crossed over the other and a shiny wingtip making agitated circles in the air. A young woman came and escorted them to a corner office.

Tremaine smiled from an executive swivel chair. Her desk was polished wood rather than the GSA metal Flores was accustomed to, although it lacked the scroll work a top ranking DC official might command. A matching credenza held a keyboard and flat screen monitor flanked by trophies from dance competitions. Behind that was a career wall of framed citations.

"Thank you all for coming," Tremaine said.

She gave them time to settle into chairs in front of the desk, content to let the authority of the environment sink in before she spoke again. Ohashi was less patient. He turned to Flores.

"Where exactly is Earl Childers?" he asked. "I mean, at this precise moment."

"Joining a health club," Flores said.

"A health club?"

"Sign up, orientation and facilities tour will take the rest of the morning." Flores had verified that with the club before she dropped Childers to attend the meeting.

"And yesterday?" Ohashi asked.

"Old car shopping and a shooting range."

Tremaine's eyes narrowed. "What sort of weapon?"

"Hunting rifle. Nothing tactical."

Flores had been curious enough to police Childers' target out of the trash barrel. It surprised her that a frail old man was a better marksman than most of the Marshals Service, at least on paper targets.

"Sport shooting," Ohashi declared, "is not terrorism. Marshall Flores, have you noticed anything in Childers' behavior that would suggest criminal activity."

Flores didn't know where Ohashi's line of inquiry was going and she didn't intend to get caught in the middle.

"The surveillance is protective, not investigative."

"Don't bother," Tremaine said. "Mr. Ohashi doesn't know the difference and he doesn't care. He is simply looking for some pretext to cancel the interview."

"The interview is unnecessary," Ohashi said.

"Not your call," Tremaine said.

"What's more, it's disruptive."

"Your people in DC have already made and lost that argument," Tremaine said. "You are welcome to observe, as agreed."

Ohashi was silent. Flores had no way to know if sulking was just part of his personality, or if something serious was troubling him.

"Marshal Flores," Tremaine said, "the Service was adamant that you also be permitted to observe the interview. You will take no notes; make no audio or video recording of the proceedings."

Those were the instructions she received from Webster. They directly contradicted Marshals Service doctrine that all activities be documented in detail, with the documents dated and signed. Webster could tell her only that word had come down from on high.

"I was briefed by the Service," she assured Tremaine.

"Mr. Weiss," Tremaine said, "you will be permitted to sit in on the interview. I would appreciate it if you could remain after the meeting so we can discuss our approach."

"Has anyone told Earl about this party," Weiss asked, "or will Marshal Flores' team just haul him in?"

"The Marshals Service surveillance will not be compromised," Tremaine said. "We are in contact with Mr. Childers' counsel. He has agreed to present himself at two PM day after tomorrow. I'd like to have all participants here at least twenty minutes early."

"Earl saw this coming," Weiss decided.

"Let's hope he also sees the value of cooperation," Tremaine said.

"Earl is smart. He figures things out fast. We need to find out exactly what he knows."

"We can discuss that later."

Tremaine looked from Ohashi to Flores and back. "Are there any questions or concerns?"

"Nothing I can expect a satisfactory response to," Ohashi said.

Flores shook her head rather than lie.

It was obvious Tremaine and Weiss knew more than they were saying, and that she could get into no end of trouble asking questions.

Several days of observing Childers had given her little on which to base an impression. He was no longer as gaunt as in the news photo, but his movements had the same deliberate measure her grandmother had been trained to use in physical therapy following her stroke. Any criminal activity would be strictly white collar.

Ohashi stood and held the door for Flores. They passed in silence through the maze of the FBI office out to the elevator lobby. The door opened on an empty car and sealed them into their own world. Ohashi's cologne had enough alcohol for an impaired driving citation.

"I was hoping for a little support from the Marshals Service," he said as the car began its slow descent. "After all, you are here at Treasury's request."

The weasel was acting like he had done her a favor. She swallowed the urge to rip him a new one. He had background on both the situation and Earl Childers. This might be her only opportunity to coax him into conversation.

She hadn't bothered putting on war paint. It wouldn't have cut any ice with Tremaine. She wasn't sure how far a fetching smile would get her with a stuffed shirt like Ohashi, but it wouldn't hurt to try.

"My assignment briefing was a little short on specifics," she said. "If you can share some information on why Childers is important to the Treasury Department, I might be able to help."

That was abrupt, but she had only a short elevator ride to score what she could. Ohashi eyed her with more than a little suspicion.

"You do know about the Hollister situation?" he asked.

She repeated the text of Bill's e-mail as closely as she could remember it. She could only hope it sounded good since she had no clue what 'in play' meant, what constituted 'leapfrog' technology, who the broker was or how much money it took to qualify as 'major'.

"Correct as far as it goes," Ohashi said with a cagey look that suggested he was wondering how much he dared elaborate.

"Hey, look, if I'm off base, say so," Flores said. "I'm completely on board with the concept of 'need to know'. If I'm not supposed to be in the loop, I don't have any issues with that. I'll just be quiet and stick to surveillance."

She hoped she sounded cooler than she felt. Where Hollister was concerned, it wasn't just curiosity. She had made the mistake of mentioning the company to Bill before she had the complete picture. Now he was hot on the trail of any opportunity he could sniff out. She needed all the information she could bluff Ohashi into giving her.

"It is public knowledge," he said, "that Hollister is poised to become a key player in industrial control software for offshore petroleum recovery."

She nodded encouragement, like she had known that all along.

"Petroleum recovery," he went on, getting comfortable as a lecturer deigning to share superior wisdom, "is an area of vital economic interest. Disruption could be catastrophic, and control software is a key vulnerability. There are rumors of an impending foreign takeover of Hollister. As a member of the firm's Board, Childers may be able to provide critical insight."

Fat chance of that. Childers had already been shunned for court testimony. He wasn't likely to turn himself into further collateral damage to satisfy random curiosity on the part of Treasury.

"Is there a specific threat?" she asked.

"That," Ohashi emphasized, "is what we are trying to ascertain."

"Have you thought about asking Tremaine to ask your questions?"

"It's not just questions," he said in a tone that dismissed Flores as hopeless. "It's an entire line of discussion."

"If no one says anything to him, he may think everything is copacetic and keep whatever he knows to himself."

Ohashi shook his head. "Childers is well off financially, but not wealthy in the modern sense. His holdings in Hollister represent at least half his net worth. If he is spooked by hostile interrogation, he may become protective, uncommunicative."

The elevator door opened on the lobby.

"Just see that Childers is kept safe," Ohashi snapped and strode out.

Flores took a moment to wrap her head around the situation. Terrorists with access to foreign military explosives had bombed a building, killing twelve people and narrowly missing Earl Childers, a member of Hollister's Board of Directors. The FBI wanted to talk to Childers about the bombing. Unspecified foreign interests were trying to take over Hollister. Treasury wanted to talk to Childers about that. The FBI and Treasury didn't want to talk to each other.

So much for a tightly integrated effort to secure the homeland. Flores rode down to the garage to retrieve her sedan and re-establish the Childers surveillance.

The more she learned about the situation, the less sense it made. The FBI insisted on interviewing Childers about a significant terrorist incident. They had the authority to bring him in immediately, but they were content to wait two days for him to come in on his own. At the same time they were going to unusual lengths to keep the content of the interview under wraps.

Treasury sounded like they had legitimate concerns about a foreign takeover of Hollister. They had been denied access to Childers. By whom no one had said, but you had to be pretty high up the food chain to tell the Treasury Department to fuck off.

Flores had been sent into the situation right off suspension, with no resources. It seemed like the Marshals Service just didn't want to get involved. They were investing only enough to keep themselves looking good, planning to cut their losses if it all blew up into something ugly. Who they might be trying to impress and what they might be afraid of were two more of a shitload of question marks.

Government was a notorious haven for people with agendas and the power to pursue them. Not always for the right reasons.

Chapter 9

*O*N THE COMFORT OF PHILIP Linfield's hotel suite, with the
soothing strains of Chopin drifting on tempered air and
colorful travel folders open on the coffee table, his plan to
confront Earl Childers had seemed a neat bit of inspiration. A meeting
at Marin Headlands Park would get them away from prying eyes. A
stroll to view Bonita Point Lighthouse would provide an opportunity
to evaluate the toll Childers' cancer had taken on his physical stamina.
Now, with the chill of the Headlands penetrating his bones as he
watched Childers make his way from the parking lot, Linfield was
having second thoughts.

On the drilling platform, Childers stayed within reach of any
available railing, as if experience had taught him his balance and strength
could falter without warning. There were no rails along Fort Barry Road.
It was just a ribbon of asphalt left over from a sprawling military base
decommissioned some half-century ago, meandering away from the old
frame church that now served as the Park Visitors Center. The terrain was
less gentle than Linfield was accustomed to in eastern parks, the sense of
isolation more pronounced. Should Childers suffer a bout of infirmity,
Linfield would have the nuisance of summoning help and the potential of
ill-will from any friends the fellow had cultivated on the Hollister Board.

"Thank you for coming," he said by way of greeting. "I hope this
isn't difficult for you."

"I promised myself a trip out here."

Perhaps Childers had come to test himself, perhaps to prove himself to Linfield. Either way, he accepted responsibility for his presence. Linfield decided the risk associated with his first instinct was worthwhile. An outdoor occasion would give him the best chance to size up the man who might endanger his plans.

To an observer, had there been one in the late hours of an overcast September morning, they might have appeared a strange pair of tourists. Two men in dress overcoats and wingtips, carrying folded-down briefcase-sized umbrellas against the distinct possibility of rain. Childers' overcoat was gray, in the herringbone pattern Linfield had always seen as provincial. The collar was turned against a raw wind off the Pacific. His scarf seemed a reasonable concession in view of his health. He was taller than Linfield, thinner and restricted to a more deliberate pace.

"How does retirement suit you?" Linfield ventured.

"I'm still adjusting," Childers said.

His tone betrayed no rancor at being exiled from a lucrative career. Perhaps age and illness had convinced him it was for the best. A faint smile suggested he was enjoying the morning's outing, in spite of the weather and any physical drain. How much of that was genuine and how much was simply an experienced negotiator's façade was impossible to tell. There seemed little to be gained from further observation. It was time to move forward.

"I will make this brief," Linfield said. "It's time you resigned from your position on Hollister's Board of Directors."

There was no change in Childers' expression. His eyes were as vague as the pockets of ground fog that drifted in the grassy fields bordering the road. It didn't seem to be a question of not hearing or understanding. Decades of the haggling involved in finance had probably given him the patience to digest surprises before he responded to them.

"I assume there is more to this than just 'here's your hat, what's your hurry'," Childers finally said.

"It's quite simple, really. The firm is being taken private."

"Buyout?"

"Soon there will be no more Board to be a member of. Now would be as good a time as any to close out your participation."

"I hadn't heard anything along those lines."

"You and the other shareholders will be paid cash for your holdings," Linfield emphasized. "You needn't worry about any complicated stock swaps or sale restrictions."

"If the Board is going away, what's the point of showing me the door?"

"Matter of convenience," Linfield said.

"It might raise questions," Childers observed. "A member of the Board's finance committee resigning just before a terminal transaction."

"Simply cite health concerns. You have overwhelming medical evidence to support your position."

"My health concerns are behind me."

That didn't ring true. Linfield's father had succumbed to cancer. He recalled ongoing medical admonitions that the disease could recur at any time without warning. Childers did not seem prone to either bravado or denial.

"Do you have other concerns?" Linfield asked. "Reasons not to leave?"

"Yesterday a former associate accused me of being paranoid," Childers said. "I didn't have any argument to offer."

"You're not suggesting that you are unbalanced?" Linfield asked.

"I'm saying I'll be happy to leave just as soon as the buyout clears escrow."

Linfield hadn't expected a direct affront to his integrity. Perhaps Childers was probing to test his temper. Best to let the subject simmer until he was in full control of his emotions.

The road brought them to an overlook. The Golden Gate Bridge stretched below in the distance, spanning the water that separated the city from the Headlands. Directly below and less spectacular was the Bonita Point Lighthouse, perched on a rock outcrop and joined to the Headlands only by a suspension bridge.

The history of the monument had caught Linfield's fancy. It was built more than a century ago as a beacon for men who risked their fortunes on every voyage of early paddle-wheel steamships. Pure capitalists who operated with no safety net at the limit of their technology, unfettered by today's web of regulation. Linfield saw himself as their direct descendant, a heritage he accepted with pride, and the Hollister acquisition as his own voyage into a sea of unlimited risk and reward.

Had he been alone, Linfield might have hiked down the rugged half-mile trail for a closer look. To watch the rollers come in off the Pacific. To smell the salt air at full tang. To imagine the kindred hopes and fears of the men who had journeyed before him. Childers had shown no ill effects so far, but the climb down and back might well over-tax him.

"Perhaps you could elaborate on your specific concerns?" Linfield inquired.

"As could you," Childers said.

"Excuse me?"

"Back in the nineteen sixties, a gentleman named Ramsay Clark was appointed Secretary of Defense. His first act was to ask to see the plan to win the Vietnam War. There wasn't one. Senior military leadership could draft no plan because senior political leadership had never defined victory in Vietnam. I left the service before Clark's time, but I helped fill body bags with the failures he uncovered. Since then, I've always made it my business to ask what was the end game and what was the strategy to achieve it. I haven't always gotten answers, and I haven't always done well with the answers I have gotten, but I have always asked."

He sounded like a man struggling to come to terms with a past he didn't fully comprehend. His antipathy toward leadership was typical of middle-class upbringing. His curiosity about the end game for Hollister wasn't. That kind of probing was the hallmark of an opportunistic professional.

"Do you think something is amiss?" Linfield asked.

"I think I'll be better positioned to inquire if I remain on the Board."

Nasal chatter carried from behind them on the road. A group of a dozen or so was approaching. In addition to being obvious tourists, they seemed to constitute some sort of extended family, less the children, who would be in school. The man in front was graying and paunchy, togged out in a raglan sport coat over a heavy sweater and an alpine hat with a small feather. A woman his age kept a pace or two behind him, nattering over her shoulder at younger couples in their thirties and forties. Speech and body language suggested a pattern. Women married safely, if not happily, and men with their last sparks of initiative being smothered under blankets of quiet desperation. Everything Linfield's soul rebelled against. He suggested to Childers that they return.

"Should you decide not to leave the Board," Linfield said when their walk had taken them out of earshot of the tourists, "the only alternative would be to put your continued membership to a vote of the other directors."

"Is it the middle-eastern money?" Childers inquired. "Are you afraid I'll ask embarrassing questions?"

Linfield had no idea how much Childers knew about his source of funds, or how he came to know it. Perhaps he was only guessing, his inquiry a stab in the dark based on some scrap of information or rumor. Questions would be counterproductive. They would only steer the fellow toward more information. In any event, Linfield would have to re-check his security.

"You stand to realize a considerable sum from the sale of your shares," Linfield pointed out. "It will all be long term capital gain, taxed at the lowest possible rate. That sort of impact on personal wealth isn't an area where any of us can afford to make mistakes."

"Financial outcome will be top of mind," Childers promised. "Mine and the other shareholders."

It was impossible to know whether Childers was stalling in the hope of lining his own pockets or whether he had genuine concern for Hollister's shareholders. The simple fact was that broader vision was required. In the balance hung world leadership in a key industrial sector; an inflow of wealth to the nation, a redress of trade imbalance and countless employment opportunities. Those who failed to grasp the overall economic realities had no role to play. The verbal sparring was over.

Linfield and Childers finished the trip back to the Visitors Center in silence.

"Thank you for the walk, Mr. Linfield. I'll need to excuse myself now. I have an appointment to make a mistake."

"Pardon me?"

"I'm on my way to pay too much for a car, to level a playing field that can't be leveled anywhere but in my own mind. We may know the principles, Mr. Linfield, and we may know how to apply them logically, but in the end we all answer to our demons."

Linfield watched the fellow make his way to the parking lot. In life as in music, there were those who enjoyed improvisation. Linfield was not among them. When the oboe blew A-Flat and the orchestra began to tune, everyone must know his part and be rehearsed to perfection.

In other circumstances, Linfield might have enjoyed bringing Childers to heel. Neither the Prince nor the precarious state of his family's government allowed time for personal amusement. If Childers refused to cooperate, measures would have to be devised.

Chapter 10

*E*ARL CHILDERS WAS COMPULSIVELY PUNCTUAL and had no patience with tardiness. Fifteen minutes of scanning the noon crowd making its way into the Food Emporium in downtown Westfield Mall left him stewing. He went to the railing where he could look down on the curving escalator that moved people between floors of shops.

Dylan Quist was two levels down, talking on his cell phone as he rode up. He seemed to be in no hurry. He strolled off the escalator and didn't end the call until a minute or so after acknowledging Childers.

"Earl, thank you for coming."

Childers resented Quist's overly familiar handclasp. "You did say it was important."

"And sensitive," Quist said. "This is something we need to discuss outside the office. And away from anyone who might take notice."

There was little chance they would attract attention in the lunch crowd. The Emporium was a large open eating area surrounded by walls of colorful vendor stalls, a jam-packed echo chamber where words were swallowed in an overwhelming buzz of conversation. The only visible danger was that Quist's histrionics would drag on until there was no table space left.

"Let's get something to eat," Childers suggested, "before all the seats are taken."

"I've got just the spot. Some of the best Italian you've ever tasted."

"This is a bad time to risk indigestion," Childers said. "I have an appointment with the FBI later this afternoon."

Quist blinked in surprise. "Anything I should know about?"

"I expect they'll tell me when I get there."

"Well, come on, then. You'll love this. Primo Italiano. Better than anything you'll find in Union Square."

"I've made my Italian mistake for the month," Childers said. "I'll get something I'm sure I can stomach and find a table."

He found a fast moving line at a teriyaki booth. Quist dogged him, ordered the same thing and insisted on paying. They located a small table.

"This conversation," Quist said, "is in strict confidence."

"What's it about?"

"I am consulting with you as a member of the Board's finance committee," Quist said. "Non-disclosure is in effect. Very definitely in effect. No one else, on or off the Board, needs to know we talked."

Childers limited himself to nodded assent. In an age where smart phones could record anything said, a verbal commitment to secrecy could come back to haunt him.

"Hollister," Quist said, "is the subject of a hostile takeover."

Hostile takeover was a commonly used term in the finance industry. It applied to a broad range of situations and might be as benign as an uninvited bid.

"Do you have any details?" Childers asked.

"Philip Linfield is planning to take the company private."

Linfield had made no secret of the buyout. Quist seemed alarmed at the prospect. Maybe he had been told something Childers hadn't.

"Has Linfield tendered an offer?" Childers asked.

"Not yet. His plan is for a Swiss Holding Company to buy out the shareholders and operate the firm as a private subsidiary."

"I don't understand the hostile part," Childers said. "Didn't you invite Linfield to the party?"

"To provide expansion funding," Quist protested. "Not to buy out the firm."

It sounded like Quist had blundered into the process with more ego than savvy and Linfield had blind-sided him.

"How much did you ask for?"

"Seven hundred fifty million dollars," Quist said, using a fork to move rice around on his plate, as if the size of the figure made him uneasy. It was three times the total value of Hollister's outstanding shares. Childers wondered how long it would take to earn back that level of investment.

"How did you arrive at that number?" he asked.

"We, that is the finance committee and I, identified all the viable expansion opportunities we had and multiplied by the projected cost of exploiting a single opportunity. You were undergoing medical treatment at the time or, of course, we would have included you."

"I wouldn't have done it any differently," Childers said. "How did you select Linfield as your funding source?"

"Only an organization of a certain size could manage that kind of financing. We made some discreet inquiries and Linfield's firm seemed the most appropriate to approach."

There was no such thing as a discreet inquiry. The finance industry's listening apparatus was tuned to pick up the slightest whisper. Linfield had seen breakthrough technology in the hands of an inexperienced CEO and smelled blood. It would be simple enough for Linfield to have his firm highly recommended and leave the impression that it was Quist who initiated contact. Childers wondered whether Quist had guessed any of that, or if he was still running on ego.

"And if you had it to do over," Childers asked, "what would you do differently?"

Quist stared for a moment. "I don't know what else we could have done at the time."

"What happened to change your mind?" Childers asked.

"Linfield is planning to offer market value of shares for the firm."

"That will add another two hundred fifty million to the amount he'll need," Childers calculated. That meant Linfield had raised a billion dollars for the project.

"Two hundred fifty million is not enough," Quist said. "Not for a company with Hollister's potential."

A billion dollars was too much to invest in firm gambling on fledgling technology. Linfield and whoever was backing him had more in mind than just a financial outcome.

"Who are his investors?"

"I told you. A Swiss holding company."

"Switzerland is just a tax haven. The fact that a company is incorporated there is meaningless."

Quist had no response. Probably he had asked no questions.

"Do we have another offer?" Childers inquired. "Or since we don't actually have this one, do we have any reason to expect anything?"

"That's why I wanted to talk to you. How do we go about generating one?"

A note of desperation came out in Quist's voice and he smiled quickly to cover it. Maybe Linfield had demanded Quist's departure as well as Childers'. In any event topping an offer that was already too large to make financial sense was all but impossible.

"I don't think we can," Childers said.

"You must have contacts," Quist insisted. "People you know from the finance industry."

The irony rankled Childers. He had forfeited a career's worth of contacts over Hollister, and now Hollister's CEO wanted to use Childers' contacts to save his own backside.

"They wouldn't touch it," Childers said. "Technology evolves rapidly. If Hollister's product doesn't get to market now, the competition will upgrade to match or exceed it. The time required to put together a viable alternative to Linfield's proposal would be longer than the firm's window of opportunity."

"You sound just like Linfield," Quist said as if he were dressing down a subordinate. "Are you ready to cave in to him?"

"I'm not suggesting we grab anything he throws on the table," Childers said.

There would be long nights poring over agreements and disclosures to exploit any opportunities and avoid any pitfalls. Childers was surprised to find that he no longer looked forward to the exercise that had defined and energized his career.

"What do you suggest, then?" Quist demanded. "If Linfield really does have us over a barrel, what's the point of even reading his submission. Why not just sign and have done with it?"

"Linfield is as much a hostage of the calendar as we are. His offer will be structured for maximum speed, and he'll give a reasonable amount of ground to keep the process on track."

The next move was Linfield's. Until he presented a formal offer, there would be nothing to discuss. Childers went back to his lunch.

Quist refused to be ignored. "We have some time. Taking a public corporation private is a complex process. It won't happen overnight."

"A team of specialists can get this done in very short order," Childers said, spearing a piece of chicken on his fork. "Look how fast the Chrysler deal went together."

"While we sit on our hands?"

"It's not about you and me. The Board exists to add value for the shareholders. Ultimately it's their call."

"You know the two largest. Better than anyone. You brought them to the firm."

The truth was that Childers knew neither man well. He had gone through his rolodex and found someone who knew a broker who was looking for a suitable situation on behalf of two potential investors.

"Nisham and Hendrick didn't put money and effort into Hollister because of me. They came chasing a dream. If they can realize it through re-capitalization, then they probably will."

"Frankly, I was hoping for a little more fight from you," Quist said.

A fight would benefit no one. What was needed was a deal everyone could live with. Childers let the subject drift.

"Talking a good game about representing the shareholders isn't enough," Quist insisted. "We need to develop some options for them."

Quist wasn't taking 'no' for an answer. Childers had no tolerance for martinets who insisted force of will would win over any obstacle. They invariably sought scapegoats when time and circumstance proved them wrong. Childers' appetite was gone. He took a last swallow of milk, pushed his chair back and stood.

"You'll have to excuse me now."

Quist stood so as to surrender as little height advantage as possible. "As Board Chairman, I will have to convene a meeting of the full finance committee."

Quist was a manager and authority was the first crutch a manager reached for. Such strengths as he had lay in routine operation and supervision. He appeared to have little financial knowledge beyond the vapid theories spoon fed at Harvard. His ego could easily make him an impediment to reaching the best available deal.

"Whatever you think appropriate," Childers said as graciously as he could manage and left Quist standing at the table.

Hollister was shaping up as an off-key swan song for his career. No gold watch and fond farewells. Just a cloud of acrimony, watching forty years swirl away like dirty water down a drain.

As problematic as Quist might be, Linfield could prove worse. Men at his level often saw themselves in the same league as the business titans of the past. Finance was a game. Winning was the objective. Profit was assumed to follow. Often it didn't. History was rife with stories of men who had played the game all the way to personal ruin. If Linfield and Quist got into it, the shareholders' fortunes, including a good portion of Childers' net worth, could hang on the actions of two men behaving irrationally.

More immediately, Childers was facing an FBI interview in an hour. He had been given no hint of the scope or subject.

Chapter 11

An FBI agent showed Valentina Flores into the viewing area, repeated Tremaine's instructions that no notes or recordings were to be made during the Childers interview and remained to ensure that Flores and Ohashi complied. Flores hoped the interview would give her some clue why a frail old man was receiving special treatment from the most arrogant law enforcement agency on the planet.

Fluorescent lights came on in the interview room, on the other side of the one-way sound-proof glass. The scrape of chairs was audible through a speaker. Tremaine and Levi Weiss sat down on one side of a small table. Earl Childers was shown in. This was Flores' first opportunity to look him over at close range. She moved to the glass for a better view.

Age had etched lines into his face and salted his hair with gray. His suit had been tailored for a modestly more robust man and betrayed some physical decline. His posture was too perfect, as if he dared not let himself relax. Flores had noticed the same thing from a distance and decided it was habit, not any apprehension over the FBI interview.

A middle-aged woman in a conservative business ensemble followed Childers. She smiled and extended a hand to Tremaine.

"Hello, Lexie. It's been a while."

"Dorrie, good to see you again. May I present Mr. Weiss, of the Attorney General's office. Levi, this is retired special agent Doreen Munn, now in private law practice."

Weiss stood and shook hands with the woman, then exchanged greetings with Childers. Everyone sat down. It was developing into a chummy gathering. Flores recalled the first principle of interviewing--build rapport with the subject--and wondered how much theater she was watching.

Munn took a tablet PC from her shoulder bag and set it on the table. "For the record, my client would like to know his status. Specifically, is he a suspect or person of interest in any criminal investigation?"

"Mr. Childers," Tremaine said, "you are here as an interviewee only. While you are not under oath, you should be aware that it is a crime to knowingly make a false statement to any Federal law enforcement officer. Your statements are being recorded for later transcription."

"I'll do my best," Childers said.

This was the first time Flores had heard his voice. It had a pleasant, collegial tone that seemed vaguely at odds with his executive bearing.

"However, my memory isn't perfect," he went on, "and I am getting on in years. If do make any errors they are not the result of any criminal intent or desire to mislead."

"That's quite a mouthful," Tremaine said with a glance at Munn.

The attorney shook her head with an innocent look.

Weiss defused the situation with a laugh. "Earl's been around the block a few times. I think what he is saying is he's not going to lie to you."

"I hope not," Tremaine said. "This is important."

She set her own tablet on the table. Visible over her shoulder was a screen full of questions, organized and numbered. The woman had done some serious preparation.

"Mr. Childers, are you, or rather were you, acquainted with the late Spenser Van Wyck?"

The name was new to Flores. With any luck, Tremaine's questions would open a window on the FBI's interest in Childers. All Flores had to do was pay attention.

Tremaine worked through inquiries establishing that Van Wyck had invited Childers to a meeting at the Savannah, but had declined to state the subject or purpose. Childers made a last minute decision not to attend due to fatigue and infirmity associated with recuperation following medical treatment.

"Did Mr. Van Wyck mention his recent trip to the Middle East?" Tremaine asked.

"No."

"Do you know why he made such a trip?"

"No."

"Or who he might have spoken with during the trip?"

"No."

Three successive denials. Same lack of inflection or emotion. Definitely not natural. Childers should at least be curious about Van Wyck's trip and why he was being asked about it. He knew more than he was saying. Apparently his definition of lying didn't extend to omission.

Tremaine went through a list of the other Savannah victims. Childers denied knowing them or anything about them. He showed no sign of recognizing any of their photos. Howard Webster's cronies doubted there was any connection between Savannah and Childers. The FBI had been interested in Childers well before the bombing. Flores began to wonder why the hell she had been sent to protect him.

"Did you witness the Savannah bombing?" Tremaine asked.

"Yes," Childers said.

"From where?"

"The hotel where I was staying at the time."

"Did it strike you as odd that you would be that close to the event?"

"No."

"Why not?"

"Urban zoning codes tend to cluster high rise residential structures."

"Can you think of any other reason?"

"No."

"Did anything at all strike you as unusual?"

Childers seemed on the verge of mouthing another automatic negative when he caught himself.

"The bomb malfunctioned," he said.

His tone suggested it wasn't as much a statement of fact as a conclusion he had reached just that second under the probing of the interview.

Tremaine shot a questioning glance at Weiss. His expression was innocent. Tremaine had revealed only that the bomb had foreign military components, and she had revealed that only to establish her jurisdiction. Flores wondered how much other information was at large, and how much Childers either knew or could guess.

"How did you come by that information?" Tremaine asked.

"I did an infantry tour in Vietnam," Childers said. "It was a long time ago, but I still remember what explosions look and sound like. If there is any amount of fire, it usually means the explosive wasn't packed correctly, and some of it burned rather than exploding."

"You remembered all that from Vietnam?"

"I spent a lot of days cooking C-rations over bits of C-4 plastic explosive. The stuff burns hot, but it is harmless unless there is a combination of heat and shock to detonate it."

"That is a remarkable amount of knowledge, Mr. Childers. Did you construct or have any part in the construction of this device?"

"No," Childers said.

"Lexie," his attorney broke in, "again, for the record, is my client suspected of any criminal activity?"

"No," Tremaine said.

Her tone was uncharacteristically resigned. Flores wondered if the questions were Tremaine's preparation or a script that had been provided for her. That might explain both the two day delay before the interview and her reluctance to follow up on an obvious lead.

Ohashi jammed his hands into his pockets.

"She's antagonizing him," he told Flores. "Exactly what I warned her not to do."

"Did you suggest any questions?" Flores asked.

"I did not," Ohashi shot back.

Tremaine returned to her list. "Mr. Childers, are you a member of the Board of Directors of a firm called Hollister?"

Ohashi blew the air out of his lungs. "That is Treasury business."

It was also FBI business, or Tremaine wouldn't be asking about it. Flores tuned out Ohashi to focus on the interview.

"Is there any activity at Hollister that might have attracted the interest of Mr. Van Wyck?" Tremaine asked.

"The firm is seeking major expansion funding."

"Have there been any overtures to or from Mr. Van Wyck or his bank in connection with the financing?"

"None that I know of."

"Who has been approached by Hollister, or made an approach to Hollister, regarding this financing?"

"Only Philip Linfield, as far as I know."

Another name Flores hadn't heard before. New players were coming out of the woodwork.

"Are you acquainted with Mr. Linfield?" Tremaine asked.

"I've met with him only once."

"What was the subject of the meeting?"

"Recapitalization of Hollister."

"Can you be more specific? Without the financial jargon, please."

"Linfield is proposing that Hollister be taken private."

"Without the financial jargon," Tremaine repeated.

"That a privately owned firm buy the publicly traded stock of Hollister from the current owners. Hollister would be removed from the public exchange. Its stock would no longer be traded. It would operate as a subsidiary of the private firm. That's the best I can do for a summary."

"And do you approve?"

"Not my call," Childers said. "It's up to a vote of the shareholders."

"You must have some opinion."

"I haven't seen the actual offer."

Ohashi strode to where Flores stood. "What the hell is she doing?" he demanded. "What does this have to do with terrorists?"

"Isn't this stuff you wanted to know?" Flores asked.

"These questions need to be asked by professionals who can craft follow-up inquiries. Not by some criminal investigator looking for dumbed-down summaries."

Ohashi went off to a corner to sulk. Tremaine finished the interview with several pages of questions about the Hollister fraud trial and whether Childers had been contacted by anyone in connection with that. When she was satisfied he hadn't, she made a few notes on her tablet.

"Thank you for your cooperation, Mr. Childers. We will let you know if we need any further information. Nothing said in this interview is to be repeated. Please communicate with this office if you intend to leave the San Francisco area."

It seemed an odd request, since Tremaine knew the Marshals Service had Childers under surveillance. She had no chance to ask about it. She had to resume surveillance, and she did not want to stick around for the coming blow-up between Ohashi and Tremaine. Her cell phone went off as she trailed Childers' Honda out of the city.

"Marshal Flores."

"Tina, it's Web. The Childers assignment is cancelled. Pack your bags and come on home."

"Say again."

"The FBI identified the target of the bombing as a New York banker. Childers is in no danger."

"Thanks, Web. You just made my day."

And maybe saved her career. She had been on the verge of being sucked into an interagency nightmare. Now job one was to get back home and warn Bill to stay away from Hollister. FBI interest left her with seriously bad vibes about that company. She took the first off-ramp to head back to the motel.

She was cramming a suitcase when the phone went off again.

"Hey, Wyatt. It's me."

"Bill? This isn't your number."

"On the road today. Any chance you can get back to the right coast for the weekend?"

"I'm on my way now. Assignment over."

"Are you up for a party? And I don't mean just a party. I mean a party."

That didn't sound like the Bill Montgomery she knew and loved. He never got excited about social events.

"Tell me about it," she said.

"That Hollister lead panned out. Big time. I've been invited to a Saturday night bash at Philip Linfield's compound."

Oh, crap. He'd already gotten himself mixed up with Hollister.

"Who is Philip Linfield?" she asked.

"Major player in private equity," Bill said. "His compound is up in Connecticut. Word is the place cost five hundred million to build. The functions there exceed anything and everything you've ever heard of."

"Taking me across state lines for immoral purposes?" She hoped.

"Seriously, Tina, this is a big deal. A real opportunity to make the right connections."

That sounded more like Bill.

"I'll call you when I get in," she said. "We'll get together and you bring me up to speed."

"Great. Gotta go now. See you."

Bill would be attending Linfield's soiree with or without her. It sounded like the other chicks there would be class ass. She would be playing defense, but at least she would be in the game.

Her big worry was Hollister. She wasn't sure what she had gotten Bill into. Treasury had their underwear in a knot. The FBI had profiled a Board member. Flores still didn't understand why the head of the Bureau's San Francisco office had interviewed Childers in person. Or why no other agency was permitted to record the interview.

There was no point asking. She was low broad on the totem pole. Nobody had to tell her shit. At least the party would be a chance to size up this Linfield character.

Chapter 12

PHILIP LINFIELD'S HELICOPTER ALLOWED HIM to respond promptly any time the rhythm of events deviated from his carefully crafted score. The machine brought him on scene with an intimidating rush of wind and noise that was probably wasted on the Prince's underlings who waited on the roof-top helipad of the Manhattan office tower where it landed. Three of them huddled at the periphery of the rotor downwash. Linfield waited until the blades idled to a stop before he opened the door and climbed down.

A woman came forward dressed in a stylish ankle-length coat. Plump oriental features were shadowed inside a protective cowl.

"I am Mrs. Yuan." She had the firm handshake of a woman accustomed to functioning in a man's world. "Welcome to New York."

"Thank you," Linfield said, trying to conceal his impatience at having to exchange pleasantries in the discomfort of a windswept roof top.

He had already been dragged half way around the world to answer one pointless summon from The Prince. A repeat episode was doubly annoying, but until he had the initial increment of project funding secured in his own account he had no choice but to comply.

Mrs. Yuan was a surprise. Her surname was Chinese and the slight inflection in her voice reminded Linfield of native Mandarin speakers he had encountered. Certainly The Prince required people who could bring a variety of language and cultural skills to his organization but there was no Chinese component to the Hollister arrangements. Linfield had no way to know what, if any, significance to attach to the fact that the Prince had selected her to greet him.

Two thugs in off-the-rack suits stood at the periphery of the helipad, looming and hulking. A pat down from one of them confirmed that The Prince was waiting below. The elevator ride gave Linfield a chance to exercise his curiosity.

"I didn't expect the privilege of meeting with His Highness again so soon," he ventured.

"A matter of national concern required his presence in this country," Mrs. Yuan said. "He was able to spare a few minutes from his schedule."

That didn't square with the urgency of the summons that had launched Linfield's hurried trip. The Prince required an immediate progress report. No funds would be released until he was satisfied. Pressing the subject with the two thugs present seemed unwise. Their English was probably limited and they might have little or no sense they were on Linfield's turf and subject to the laws of his country.

The elevator opened on a windowless hallway, softly lit and thickly carpeted. The few doors were solid wood, closed against intrusion, displaying only generic names and meaningless logos. The sort of environment where business could be conducted away from prying eyes. Mrs. Yuan stopped at a door and swiped a magnetic security card. The name was in Arabic and Linfield's best translation was some sort of Islamic charity.

A handsome Semitic youth dressed too nattily for his position behind the reception desk greeted them with a smile.

"Please make yourselves comfortable. His Highness will be available shortly."

The chairs offered more in the way of matching décor than comfort but any hospitality had to be graciously accepted. Linfield surrendered his topcoat and sat down.

Mrs. Yuan shed her overcoat. Neither her dress nor hairstyle would have been out of place at a PTA meeting. She had a motherly countenance that went with herding a brood of children.

"Can I get you something while you wait?"

"No," Linfield said, adding, "thank you," so he wouldn't sound cross at being made to wait.

"Some tea, perhaps?" she persisted.

Linfield didn't need some alien concoction on top of the anxiety churning in his stomach. He smiled and shook his head.

Mrs. Yuan settled herself in a companion chair. The thugs remained standing. No one spoke. A faint scent of mimosa drifted on subtle currents of tempered air. The office music had a distinctly mid-eastern flavor; woodwind overtones that conjured images of unschooled shepherds making a bad job of playing parochial flutes.

Presently a man strode out into the reception area. He had the densely muscled build favored by the Prince for his bodyguard, but this fellow's suit fit properly. His carriage and the cadence of his gait were military. Close-cropped hair and a weather-worn face left him looking distinctly out of place in the offices of a charity. A scar ran down from the corner of one eye to create the illusion of a permanent tear.

The two thugs came to sloppy imitations of attention. The man passed without a sideways glance and went out into the hallway. After minute soft chimes announced that an elevator had come to remove him.

The receptionist smiled. "His Highness will receive you now."

Mrs. Yuan led the way along an interior passage flanked on one side by closed offices and on the other by cubicles of staff people. She knocked respectfully on an office door.

"Come." The Prince's voice, sharp and peremptory.

The office was a corner location, midway up in the building, neither large nor pretentious, offering no view beyond neighboring skyscrapers. The décor was predictably middle-eastern, with tapestry instead of framed oils on the walls and an ornate rug with polished hardwood visible at the edges. Unlike his previous encounter, Linfield found The Prince alone. This was a new situation and he would have to feel his way carefully.

The Prince sat behind a carved desk that called to mind days when British civil servants ruled over vast Arab fiefdoms. The Bedouin regalia were gone. His meaty jowls were clean shaven, his tailoring Saville Row. A slim-line laptop occupying his attention made it clear these were temporary quarters. He did not look up when Linfield entered.

Linfield carried no briefcase this time, only a practiced air of quiet confidence. Mrs. Yuan indicated a chair set before the desk and Linfield seated himself. The woman stood behind his left shoulder. One of the thugs stood behind Linfield's right shoulder. The Prince closed his laptop.

"Good morning, Mr. Linfield. I hope we have not inconvenienced you?"

"I am at your service, Your Highness."

The Prince considered him for a minute without seeming to come to any definite conclusion. "I wonder why you do not make your headquarters on Wall Street, where you could keep your finger on the pulse of finance."

Linfield did his best to veil his disgust at the idea. For all its panache, Wall Street was little more than over-compensated salesmen hawking secondary paper and bloated banks that had lost sight of their primary role as lenders and facilitators. It was a culture where prostitution was epidemic, cocaine consumption had reached industrial levels and no one bothered to look past the next bonus. None of that would interest the Prince. Best to tell him what he wanted to hear.

"Wall Street is a chatty environment, Your Highness. My clients require the utmost discretion."

"Do you have a date by which you expect to complete the Hollister acquisition?" The Prince asked.

His abrupt change of subject was undoubtedly meant to convey some sort of displeasure. It might be investor's nerves; the last minute case of jitters before money was actually released and control relinquished. Linfield offered a reassuring smile.

"I have personally conducted the final assessment and delivered the preliminary notifications. We can tender the offer and begin the process as soon as the funds are on deposit."

"I did not ask when you would begin. Do you not understand the word complete?"

The fellow's stare would have done justice to the strictest schoolmaster. It was pure theater. He had been rigorously trained in finance. He knew that no cash offer could be tendered without evidence of funds on deposit or letter of credit. And experience would have left him intimate with the complexities to be dealt with once the offer was in place.

"One month following funding," Linfield proposed.

"Three weeks," The Prince shot back. "I will not allow American law firms to pad their fees with funds held in trust for my people."

The last bit was nonsense. Middle-eastern royalty had prattled about being beneficent rulers all the way back to *The Arabian Nights*. In fact the general population was an after-thought in the best of times and a security concern in the worst. Linfield nodded understanding. The fellow could make of that what he wanted.

"What opposition have you encountered?" the Prince asked.

"Nothing unexpected, Your Highness."

"Be specific."

"There is always an entrenched minority that resists change."

"Minorities can be strident."

"Not if the proper pressures are applied."

"Discretion," The Prince emphasized, "remains a paramount concern."

Linfield wondered if that was why they were meeting in the offices of a charity rather than one of the several of The Prince's ventures with business quarters in Manhattan. And if it was, whether The Prince was trying to conceal the transaction from hostile elements in his own country.

"I have recruited a special team for the project," Linfield assured him. "Respected members of the financial community. Men of spotless professional reputation from fine families. Their activities will attract no attention."

It was more of the sort of thing Linfield imagined nervous royalty liked to hear, and the Prince seemed satisfied. Linfield didn't mention that he had invited the project team to mingle with his staff at a semi-formal function at his compound; just to be sure none were prone to social indiscretion. As uneasy as The Prince was, that seemed a doubly good precaution.

The Prince opened his laptop. "I will authorize release of the first increment of funding. I will expect your commitments to be met."

"Thank you, Your Highness."

The Prince busied himself with the computer. The meeting was over. Mrs. Yuan escorted Linfield out to the elevator lobby.

"His Highness is placing a great deal of trust in you," she said with a combination of admiration and apprehension.

She was fishing for any hint of trouble that he hadn't confided to The Prince, and doing it with a level of subtlety a cut above the usual lickspittles who conducted the fellow's business.

"I will strive to exceed his expectations," was all Linfield promised.

The elevator ride to the roof gave Linfield a chance to process the meeting. It would be easy to dismiss the Prince's anxiety as a normal reaction to the scope and risk of the investment. Linfield had to keep his own nerves in check. But that didn't square with his experience. When middle-eastern players grew nervous, their instinct was to haggle. Bargaining was part of their culture. Lower the price, raise the payout or both. The Prince had done none of that.

Linfield sensed desperation. Perhaps a pressing need to get the funds buried where inquisitors could not reach them in the event things went badly in The Prince's homeland. Linfield had to consummate the buyout before either cold feet or hot pursuit cost him the months and the millions he had invested in the project and dashed his hopes for its outcome. Obstacles would have to be overcome by any means necessary.

Chapter 13

$\mathcal{E}$ARL CHILDERS WAS SUDDENLY AWAKE with the taste of fear sharp in his mouth. A high-pitched buzz tortured his ears. A red strobe flashed at irregular intervals, casting grotesque shadows on the walls of his bedroom. The intrusion alarm had gone off. The piercing noise and flickering brilliance overwhelmed his senses and he could think of nothing but shutting them off. He rolled out of bed, stiff from an ambitious health club visit, gained a semblance of balance and made his way to a console set into the wall.

The glowing touch screen was unfamiliar and the instructions were fuzzy in his mind. He had to squint without his glasses. It was a minute before darkness and silence rewarded his experiments.

Childers had taken pains to make sure the alarm system worked, but had not thought about what he would do in an actual situation. After a life in urban apartments and condominiums, the quiet of the suburbs and the cavernous interior of the house were an alien environment. The alarm might and have driven an intruder to ground. Some jittery drug addict waiting in the darkness, ready to lash out in panic or rage at any light or movement. He stood still, listening, shivering a little.

His eyes began to adjust. Ambient neighborhood light filtered through the high windows and brought with it wavering shadows. A brief tinkle of wind chimes explained the movement. Maybe something outside had triggered the alarm. One of the raccoons he had seen down by the greenbelt. Or neighbor kids with time on their hands and too little supervision. His heart rate subsided and he retrieved his glasses from the night stand.

He was cursing himself for an overactive imagination when his conversation with the security company representative came to mind. A signal would have registered in the local company facility. The police would have been notified immediately. They would show up in the dead of night under a full head of adrenaline, ready for anything. Childers was liable to be shot by some well-intentioned soul coming to his rescue. He needed to defuse the situation. Have the yard lights on when the police arrived. Be ready to open the remote control gate at the head of the driveway.

The nearest controls for the yard lights were in the study that adjoined his bedroom. He padded barefoot in his pajamas, navigating by ambient light. Light moving outdoors made patterns between the slats of the mini-blind shading the study window. The shadows in the room were still. The wind chimes were silent. Stiff legs carried Childers to the window. He stood to one side and turned the wand that angled the slats in the blind to peer out.

Someone was using a flashlight at the end of the driveway, just outside the gate. This was no false alarm.

Seen by day the gate was imposing, wrought iron bars rising eight feet and topped by a row of spikes, hinged to a brick post on one side and locked by an electrically controlled mechanism to a matching post on the other, part of a fence that surrounded the yard. The fence was shrouded in thick shrubbery that allowed no view either of or from the street and blocked much of the light that originated there. Childers had to match shapes and shadows to his recollection of the landscape.

Someone had backed what looked like a commercial van into Childers' driveway, close to the gate. Between the gate and the rear of the van were two figures, more silhouettes than people. One held the flashlight while the other tried to work a pry bar into the locking mechanism of the gate.

Fear came slowly this time, creeping like ice up Childers's spine. The intruders must have heard the alarm. If they were still bent on mischief, they were either desperate or drug-addled. Perhaps both. Childers had a vision of the police dawdling in some coffee shop, thinking this was just another nuisance. He needed to call 911.

The telephone was on the desk, on the other side of the window. Any movement might alert the two figures at the gate. He made the trip on his hands and knees, careful to stay below the sill.

Bright light came suddenly through the blind and cast lattice-work shadows on the walls. A car was moving on the street that curved past Childers' house. The high beams would distract the intruders. Childers lifted his head just high enough to see over the sill.

The flashlight was out. The two figures crouched behind the van, waiting for the car to pass. The car didn't pass. It stopped with its high beams trained on the front of the van. Red and blue strobes sent hobgoblins dancing in the hedge that hid the street from Childers' sliver view of events.

An amplified voice broke the stillness. "Police. Stop what you are doing. Show me your hands."

The situation didn't look right. There was no line of sight from the rear of the van to the police cruiser. That meant there must be at least one more intruder near the front of the van, invisible to Childers but in sight of the officer on the street. The officer probably had no idea there were two men behind the van.

"Show me your hands. I need to see your hands."

One of the figures at the rear of the van began to move. A man in a shiny outer garment that shifted color in time to the pulse of the emergency strobes, like the reflective scales of a reptile slithering across a rock. He slipped around to the side of the vehicle, disappearing from Childers' view. The hedge growing up to the brick gateposts would conceal the movement from the officer on the street. Childers reached under the window blind so he could release the latch and shout a warning.

The latch was unfamiliar and wouldn't respond to his efforts. The amplified voice remained calm and authoritative, relying on presence and persistence to gain control of the situation.

"Show me your hands. I need to see--"

The pop of a pistol came, sudden and distinct, like a cork releasing out of a champagne bottle. The exchange that followed was a mix of pistol and rifle fire, sharp and sporadic. It lasted less than a minute and died away into a following silence that gave no hint of the outcome.

The strobes cast light and color and shadow into the room, dancing a syncopated samba on the walls and masking any visual clue to what might be happening outside. Childers raised the blind cautiously, managed to release the window latch and slid the pane open a few inches, staying to one side and listening.

"You get him, man?"

The voice came from near the gate. It was tense, demanding.

"I don't know, man," came a second voice.

"What you mean, you don't know?"

"I can't see shit."

"So look."

"I can't see shit. Lights in my eyes. I can't see shit."

"Well, just go over and fucking look."

"I ain't going over there, man. Fucking cop's still got his shit on him."

"Just go look."

"I ain't getting shot."

"Just fucking go."

"You go. You're the big fucking leader. You go look."

A third voice came, higher pitched and full of nerves. "Quit fucking around. We got to split."

"Fuck that. We gotta take care of business."

"Man, you crazy. More cops be coming. We gotta haul ass."

"We take care of business. Fucking Chinaman don't pay if we don't, so we take care of business."

"How we gonna get in there?"

"Get up on top of the truck. Jump over the fucking fence."

"I can't jump that far."

"Just get your ass up on the truck. We back it up."

Childers had no doubt that his murder was the business. He did not understand why anyone would want to kill him. Why anyone would pay to have him killed. He knew no one called the Chinaman. The possibility that it might be some nightmare mistake crossed his mind only briefly. He had seen the Savannah go up in flames not two blocks from his hotel. He had escaped death then. Someone had come tonight perhaps to rectify that error. He had nowhere to run. This was his sanctuary. He would have to stand his ground.

The old Winchester lay in its case on a shelf a few feet from where he crouched. He dragged the case back to the window, moving on his hands and knees, and raised his head just enough to glance out.

Two figures were boosting a third onto the roof of the van. Childers' fingers trembled with age and nerves. Darkness didn't help his efforts to release the clasps on the rifle case. The weapon was wrong way around when he pulled it out.

The van began to back, slowly, so the man on top could stay balanced. When the van touched the gate, the man would be able to jump over. Childers opened the rifle's action and fumbled a single round into the chamber. He locked he action and pushed the muzzle of the Winchester out the window.

The van stopped.

"Jump over," a voice ordered. "Do your business."

There was enough light from the street to allow crisp sight alignment but Childers was shaking too badly to hold it.

"Ain't you coming?" a second voice asked.

"Just jump over and do your fucking business."

Childers braced against the window frame, immobilizing himself to steady the rifle, and focused on thinking the trigger straight back. The recoil startled him. He jerked back from the window to avoid any return fire.

Muzzle flash had destroyed the remains of his night vision. The blast took his hearing. He had no way to evaluate what the shot had accomplished. All he could do was work cartridges into the loading port of the Winchester. The weapon was no match for the intruders' rapid firing arsenal. It was a curio, bought solely for sentiment. The single round Childers fired had certainly given away his position. He chambered a fresh round and sent his mind scrambling through his options.

The yard lights represented as much risk as hope. He had never used them. Even if he could sort out the controls, they were as likely to make a target of him as to frighten away the intruders. Abandoning his position meant making his way through a still unfamiliar house. Any noise would compromise him. The intruders would know where he was, but he might have no idea where they were.

If he stayed put, the intruders would be forced to come to him. They would cast shadows in the flickering light and make noise in the low hedge outside the window. There was nothing to do but wait. Wait as he had decades earlier when parachute flares broke the jungle night, wondering if fate had chosen this as his last day on earth.

Chapter 14

*V*ALENTINA FLORES WISHED SHE HAD brought flat heeled shoes. Normally stilettos were an advantage when she was out with Bill. Heels reduced their height difference and gave her an edge over any women with ideas. She hadn't expected the hike from the parking area of Linfield's compound to the main building.

"The property covers twenty six acres," Bill was saying. "Eleven buildings in all."

He had been waxing eloquent about the Linfield Empire since they left DC. Flores had tuned him out. Her years in the Service had taught her to rely on her own observations.

The two of them were part of a parade of guests moving up a decorative gravel path flanked by manicured shrubbery. The couple ahead was the standard manager chick/loser boyfriend combination. She was a tall, thin forty. He was a twenty-something gym rat who didn't spend enough time in Neimann Marcus overcoats to look comfortable in one. He wouldn't need to dress up to stroke her ego, cut the wear and tear on her vibrator and whatever else it took to make her feel successful and naughty at the same time.

The stone manor ahead did its best to scream success, looming three stories against a backdrop of gathering dusk, showing enough decorative lead in the window panes to send the EPA into convulsions and still falling short of the intended effect. The attending shrubbery had lost its blooms for the year. The only color came from the changing leaves of deciduous trees that would soon be skeletons in the coming northeast winter, a chilling suggesting that these might be the last glory days.

A broad staircase rose to double doors that let them into a vast two story entry floored in elegant parquetry. The coat room was as big as Flores' apartment.

"Cozy little cottage," she remarked, but Bill was too enthralled by his surroundings to pay any attention.

She didn't recognize any of the people crowding the entry. That was a relief. She wouldn't be carrying the usual occupational baggage. Word travelled fast when she was spotted. Watch what you say girls. Anything can be used against you. And leave the party favors in your purses if you don't want to get busted.

Nametags were individually made by a calligrapher. The formal reception line would be Flores' chance to eyeball Linfield up close and personal. She followed Bill, practicing her handshake and polishing her smile.

Linfield was younger than she expected, not yet fifty, and trim for his age, as if he kept a rowing machine in his office. His tailoring was impeccable. He had an easy smile and a handshake that was firm without being overbearing. The manner was too good to be natural and beneath the cultivated exterior she sensed the coiled energy of a predator who would bare his teeth quickly if he didn't get his way.

"A pleasure to meet you, Ms. Flores," he said in a voice that had been coached to perfect pitch and modulation.

"Thank you, Sir. I've heard a great deal about you."

She hoped she was projecting the right level of enthusiasm. Linfield's scrutiny suggested she was being carefully checked for social suitability.

"Do you work with Bill?"

"My field is law."

Bill hadn't specifically asked her not to say she was a Deputy US Marshal, but she had decided everyone would be more comfortable if she kept it generic. Linfield was probably just probing for acceptable phrasing and didn't care what the answer was.

"I do hope you will enjoy our little gathering," he said.

Next in line was Linfield's wife. Harriet, according to her nametag. She was in her element, born to the elite, with a hostess' smile and a watchdog's eyes. Flores was glad to make it past without drawing more than a limousine liberal's look of condescension.

The reception line ended in a huge parlor. The walls were paneled and hung with framed oils of town and country scenes that encouraged visitors to imagine themselves at home among the rich and powerful. People mingled and conversations blended into a hum. Servers in tuxedos toured with trays of fluted champagne glasses. A pianist in an evening gown set a convivial mood.

This was the meet-and-greet portion of the evening, and Bill was determined to expand his range of contacts as widely as possible. The result was a whirlwind hour of grin and skin with a paranoid undercurrent of people sizing each other up to see what threat they might pose and how they could be used. It was a Type-A shark tank. Flores hoped Bill wasn't getting in over his head.

Dinner was buffet style. White coated servers stood ready to carve meat. More shuttled trays of entrée choices, iced pans of shrimp and a variety of appetizers. Linen and silver service waited for the guests in the dining hall. Wines were decanted to taste. Flores wondered how many dinner gaffes it was possible for her to commit without realizing she had goofed.

Table talk ranged from discussions of which private schools produced the best academic and social results to tax relief on carried interest and the appropriate risk premium for oil speculation. Flores focused on smiling and nodding and hoped she didn't come off as a complete cluck.

Linfield addressed the group when they were finished, thanking everyone for their hard work and introducing the new team that would be handling the Hollister privatization. Bill stood with several others and received polite applause.

"This transaction," Linfield said, "represents the largest single venture ever undertaken by this firm. The reputation and influence that accrue to successful execution will open opportunities far beyond the fees and equity we garner from a single project. This will be the springboard from which we catapult into the future."

Flores wondered where Ohashi had come up with his concerns about a foreign takeover of Hollister. This was an All-American snob-fest. It was time to stop playing Deputy US Marshal and get serious about her personal life. She would never get a better shot at turning Bill's head.

The evening finished with dancing. Live music was provided by an eight piece band. Linfield took a turn on piano, a Yamaha grand that probably cost as much as an SUV. He was good, and he got a visible rush out of playing.

Bill knew the basic ballroom combinations from his days at an upper crust prep school and he could do a reasonable cha-cha, but when it came to the jive, he needed to find the men's room. Since Linfield was tickling the ivories, Flores decided there was nothing wrong with going up-tempo. A little jealousy wouldn't hurt her cause. She spotted a cute hunkie who obviously had some training and a dumpy partner who was demurring. She had put down enough champagne to move in.

"Dance, sailor?"

It was a dumb-ass line, but it had worked for Lena Olin when she picked up Robert Redford in *Havana*. The poor guy was startled, and she had him on the floor before he was really aware. The song was the competition standard *Shake, Rattle and Roll* and two minutes of it left both of them panting. Flores had no idea what possessed her to think she could still do a decent sugar push after all these years off the floor. Bill was back and she was glad to return to being a lady, foxtrot, five point hold and all.

The festivities broke up a little after midnight. The walk down to the car was no fun balancing on stilettos with her head buzzing but she made it and it was up to Bill to get them to the motel.

*   *

Flores knew from the ring tone that it was her cell phone. "Bill, are you awake."

"I am now."

"Pass me the phone, will you?"

"Do you really need it?"

"Come on, Bill. It's not going to stop."

The mattress undulated beneath her as he turned over and handed her the phone. She shook the cobwebs and the residue of champagne out of her head.

"Marshall Flores."

"Tina, it's Web. Sorry about the hour."

"I'll survive. What is it?"

"I need you on the first thing flying to San Francisco. Use your badge to bump someone if you have to."

"Childers?" she asked.

"Somebody took a run at him about an hour ago."

"What do you mean, took a run at him?"

"Automatic weapons. Two dead. That's all I know. San Francisco will handle things until you arrive."

"What do they need me for?"

"Right now, this situation is somebody else's screw up. The Marshal's Service was pulled off. We had nothing to say about it. When we go back, we have to look like we're going with the same team to serve notice to the world that we had the right combination from the beginning."

Flores rolled her eyes, but didn't interrupt Webster.

"Do not, under any circumstances, tell anyone you were the only Marshal on Childers the first go around. If anybody asks about composition of the original detail, refer them to me. And don't waste time telling me that's bureaucratic bullshit. It's the way it is and it is not going to change."

"Okay, okay, I'm all over it."

"And Tina, when you get to San Francisco, Lexie Tremaine is running things."

"What things, Web?"

"I don't know. I don't even know anybody who knows. Just don't get into it with her over anything. If there is a problem, call me."

"Yes, Sir."

"And one more thing." Webster's voice softened. "You're going back in because I know you can handle it."

"Thanks, Web," she said, and hung up.

She flopped back on the mattress and found Bill's hand. He gave a gentle squeeze.

"Gotta go?" he asked.

"I'm really sorry. Do me a favor and call a cab while I get dressed."

"I'll drive you."

"No. You get some sleep. This is business."

"Tina, you're not getting into a taxi alone at three thirty in the morning."

"Bill, I'm a Deputy US Marshall. I carry a badge and a gun. I eat trouble for lunch."

"I'll drive you."

"God, you sound like my father."

"I take that as a compliment."

She rolled over and sat up. He sat beside her.

"Look, Tina, I know I get wrapped up in my career. Before I know it, the days have flown by and there was no time for anything else. But on the few occasions I get, I would like to be there for you."

He put an arm around her shoulders.

She managed a quick, "thanks," before she stood and made a beeline for the bathroom so he wouldn't see that she was tearing up. Perfect timing. Her personal life was just starting to click and up popped her professional life and turned it into a train wreck.

Chapter 15

PHILIP LINFIELD RETREATED TO THE sanctuary of his den and sank into his favorite chair. Loosening his tie and unfastening his collar button eased the drum beat that pulsed in his head. He was too wired to sleep. Time drifted without measure as he gathered his thoughts from the fog of exhaustion that followed the reception.

Since his return from San Francisco he had grown increasingly concerned that his organization had been infiltrated. It didn't seem possible that Earl Childers could have guessed the source of the Hollister funding. Nor did Childers have the resources to mount a campaign of industrial espionage. That meant not only was information being siphoned out, but it was leaking into the public domain, at least as far as Childers' contacts.

The reception line had given him a look at everyone connected with the organization, a chance to size them up along with their significant others. Nothing stood out in his memory. The whole affair had the treadmill sameness of a thousand other receptions, until the dancing. One couple in one dance clearly were, or had once been, professionals. Professional dance was ill-paid, physically demanding and not commonly found in the background of people in finance.

The woman was probably trivial. She was the girl-friend of the young Montgomery fellow. He was being recruited as temporary staff for the Hollister acquisition, not yet a formal member of the organization, and had no access to information. The fellow she had danced with was another matter. He had come with a younger member of the permanent staff. A girl with intellectual promise but not physically attractive and not yet paid enough to afford a toy boy. He would have to be checked.

A knock on the door interrupted Linfield's thoughts.

"Come," he said, and regretted sounding like The Prince.

The man who stepped in was one of the duty people. Linfield's organization had grown too big to remember names. That wasn't a good sign. Loyalty depended on a sense of community. He would have to look at everything, top to bottom. Streamline operations. Seal the firm against future leaks. For now, he would have to see to matters at hand.

"What is it?" he inquired.

"Mr. Linfield, you asked to be notified in person as soon as the Beirut account was funded."

It was Sunday in Lebanon. The banks would not be open for business, but computers would be turning over. Moving The Prince's money had been as simple as two machines talking to each other. God help the world's financial network if the computer system ever broke down, or fell victim to sabotage.

"Amount?" Linfield snapped.

"The full two hundred fifty million dollar initial installment, as expected."

Adrenaline surged through Linfield's system. His moment had come. He could finally set the Hollister acquisition in motion.

"Sit down," Linfield ordered. "Take notes."

The man sat at the front of a chair cushion and poised his fingers over a tablet PC on his lap. At least Linfield also would be able to move at electronic speed.

"I want the Gulfstream ready. San Francisco. Non-stop."

"Timing, Sir?"

"Now. I do not pay people to sleep."

"Yes, Sir."

"Notice to all members of the Hollister acquisition team. Prepare for immediate deployment to San Francisco. Duration to be determined."

"Yes, Sir."

"Notice to Travel and Facilities. San Francisco office space ready for occupancy Monday. Ticketing and accommodations for all Hollister acquisition team members in place."

"Yes, Sir."

"Mark all notices urgent. Everyone is 24/7 until this is complete."

Linfield dismissed the fellow with a wave. His mind was already arranging his next moves.

The noise of the door broke his train of thought. Hattie came in, a silk lounging robe replacing the god-awful gown she had insisted on wearing for the reception. Her hair was tousled. He wondered if she had gone to bed and awakened in one of her night sweats. She crossed the room with ominous steps that served notice her hormones were running high.

"How long will you be gone this time?" she asked.

It wasn't a question of abandonment. Hattie and her cronies had no qualms about spending a four day weekend in New York, commiserating their way through menopause. The issue was supervision. She had her household allies, watching when she was gone. While he was in San Francisco she would be blind to his activities.

"As long as the acquisition requires," he said.

"Did it occur to you that I might like to go along on one of your little company hunting safaris?" She sat on the arm of his chair and danced her fingertips on his shoulder. "We could have some fun in San Francisco. See the sights. Spend some time together."

"Hattie, it's not a nine to five job. Any absence on my part, any loss of focus, could have repercussions."

She withdrew her hand and her voice hardened. "Your precious position might be threatened?"

"My position is your position, Hattie."

"I wish you would remember that," she said, "next time you feel like embarrassing both of us by hammering on a piano like some sophomore music prodigy."

He and Hattie had met in college. She had banged a few upperclassmen back in the day and never gotten past the notion that made her an expert on all subjects social, from relationships to propriety.

"Activities like tonight's are meant to foster closeness with the staff," he said.

"I don't recall my father requiring that sort of antic to keep his people in line."

It seemed forever ago that Hattie had been the intersection of Linfield's passion and his ambition. She had turned him into the kind of love-struck swain he had always regarded with contempt. Her father was the disapproving patrician cliché which, coupled with Hattie's sense of rebellion, drove her closer to Linfield.

Linfield had courted them both relentlessly then, but eventually the old man drifted into dotage and passing years took their toll on the marriage.

Hattie's family connections had been invaluable when he was starting. Now that he was the established financial force, her relatives were becoming more of a drag than an asset. Over-privileged loafers for the most part. It seemed she pestered him constantly for job recommendations, introductions and the occasional loan for them. The touch of her fingers had been used too often to manipulate him, and had forfeited any attraction. Linfield stood and went to the sideboard.

"Would you like something to drink?"

"You will need to set an example for Kit and Susan," she insisted.

The kids were away in college now. Kit would graduate next spring and join the firm for two or three years' seasoning before he would be packed off to Carnegie Mellon for his MBA. Susan was talking about declaring a pre-law major, but Linfield thought she would probably follow her mother and show up on the doorstep with some ambitious young stud in tow. Hopefully the fellow could make himself useful. In any event, both children were too old and independent for Hattie to use them as a cudgel any longer. Pointing that out would only draw another tirade.

Linfield had found the solution in music. There was no cacophony so obnoxious that it did not have some use, and he had, over the years, pieced together a mix that set Hattie's nerves on edge. He scrolled down the play list on the touch screen embedded in the wall and tapped a finger on the surface.

Speakers built into the bookshelves came to life. The room reverberated to the beat of Cannibal and the Headhunters' *Land of a Thousand Dances.*

Hattie stood and stalked out.

Little remained for her to contribute. The time was coming when her role would have to be re-evaluated. Linfield took his cocktail back to the chair and opened his laptop. He brought up the evening's guest list and then touched out a number on his phone.

"My God, Phillip," came a groggy response. "Do you ever sleep?"

"You don't have a God, Elmer. And sleep is a luxury not even the old rich can afford any more."

"If you're calling a lobbyist at this time of night on your private line, it can't be good news. What am I supposed to do? Buy you a Supreme Court decision?"

"Nothing that dramatic," Linfield assured him. "I may have an industrial espionage issue."

Linfield read the name of his employee and her escort, spelling them so Elmer could copy correctly. He listened to himself explain his suspicions and wondered if he were growing paranoid. Childers had mentioned paranoia. Perhaps it was an occupational affliction.

"I need you to locate an investigation firm," he told Elmer. "Discreet. Well connected. No ties to the finance industry. Neither the suspects nor anyone in my organization, nor the industry, should be aware there is an inquiry."

"Philip, that's time, effort, surveillance."

"As you know, I have a particularly big iron in the fire just now."

"Hollister," Elmer said in a voice grown weary of the subject.

Linfield had not heard even a rumor of competition involving the Hollister deal, but if someone were planning something underhanded, they might well seek to penetrate his organization, as well as recruit assistance from Earl Childers.

"I need facts," he said as much for his own benefit as Elmer's. "Who has commissioned this and why."

"Not that I don't appreciate the work, Philip, but wouldn't it be quicker and cheaper just to fire this broad's ass?"

"Elmer, not only have you no God, you also have no imagination. Whoever commissioned the espionage is not going away. If their first attempt fails, they will be back with something more sophisticated. They have to be rooted out and dealt with."

"What about the other broad? The one this character was dancing with?"

"She came with a new hire contractor. No access to information."

"This contractor will have to be given information at some point," Elmer said. "Are you sure she isn't hooking up with him as a new source?"

"No, I'm not sure," Linfield realized.

If the target of the espionage was Hollister, they would need a source on the acquisition team. Linfield cursed himself for not seeing that at once. He scrolled through the guest list.

"Flores," he said. "The name is Valentina Flores. Check her also."

"Okay, Philip. Wire ten large to the Cayman account. I'll get the ball rolling."

Linfield ended the call and used his laptop to transfer the funds. The Hollister acquisition was shaping up as a stress test for both him and his organization; a priceless opportunity to learn what they could do and where they needed to improve. It would demand that he restructure the firm and re-focus his personal life to take advantage of the opportunities that lay ahead.

"Game on," he said, and used the remote to recue Cannibal and the Headhunters.

Chapter 16

$\mathcal{E}$ARL CHILDERS STOOD FOR A minute watching a police forensic team scour the area at the end of his drive. The gate hung crookedly on its hinges. Yellow crime scene tape held back a couple of gawkers out jogging in the dawn haze. Childers shivered in spite of a heavy cardigan and closed the door.

Doreen Munn shed her parka. Slacks, a casual top and minimal makeup indicated she had put herself together quickly after receiving his call. She tossed her head to free a comb out hair-do and carried a shoulder bag and a Styrofoam coffee cup into the living room.

"What happened?" she asked, sitting on the sofa.

The question, combined with her worried look, told Childers he didn't look any steadier than he felt. He lowered himself into a chair facing her with an uneasy glance at the smart phone she set on the coffee table to record their conversation.

"The intrusion alarm went off and triggered a police response. There was some shooting. I think the intruders got away."

"Have the police talked to you?" she asked.

"They made me identify myself. Went through the house with flashlights and guns. Poked around the yard. I don't think they found anything."

"Did they tell you what happened on the street?"

Childers knew only what he had seen and heard. The van had fled at the sound of approaching sirens. To avoid spooking the police, he had turned on the yard lights, put the Winchester back in its case and locked it up.

"All they said was to stay in the house," he told Munn.

Emergency presence on the street grew to massive proportions. A helicopter prowled the sky, probing with its searchlight. The four AM news had a sound bite alerting the audience to a breaking story. He had called Munn only for legal advice, to ask if there was anything special he should do. He hadn't expected her to come in person.

"The first officer on scene suffered multiple gunshot wounds," Munn said. "He arrived at the hospital with no vital signs. They were not able to resuscitate."

"I'm sorry," Childers said.

It sounded inadequate. He had seen the ambulance pull away and let himself believe that everything would be all right. Survivor guilt began to gnaw at him.

"I had a talk with the Sheriff's Lieutenant who is supervising the scene," Munn said.

"What did he say?"

"Probably more than he should have. He remembered me from an investigation back in the day. Your intruders' van was found abandoned. One man was dead inside. He had a felony arrest record."

The police hadn't asked whether Childers had done any of the shooting. The odor of burned nitro powder had dissipated by the time they searched the house. Either they hadn't noticed the rifle case or hadn't thought it worth investigating.

"What do the police think?" he asked.

"What they were meant to think. That this was a home invasion robbery gone bad."

"Meant to think?"

"Earl, if I am to represent you effectively, I need to know everything, and I need to know it now."

Her tone was grave, her eye contact demanding. The abrupt change in attitude startled Childers.

"What do you think I'm holding back?" he asked.

"You didn't tell me that you had requested Federal witness protection."

"Because I hadn't."

"Earl, I have a law practice to protect. I can't continue to represent you unless I have all the facts."

Munn had not come to provide legal advice. She had come to assess the risk he represented as a client.

"I have had two conversations with Federal law enforcement," he said. "The first was the call I made following the Savannah firebombing, which I told you about. The second was my FBI interview, which you attended and which was why I retained you."

"I still have a few friends in the system," she said. "I called in a favor and learned that the US Marshals Service had your back until two days ago."

Childers replayed his call to the government in his mind. He remembered nothing to indicate which agency had answered. No indication that he would receive any protection or monitoring.

"Why did they stop?" he asked.

"I don't know. Have you spoken to Levi Weiss about protection?"

"I haven't spoken to Levi since the Hollister trial. I was surprised when he showed up for the FBI interview. I thought he worked in Manhattan."

"Do you know who Levi Weiss is?" Munn asked.

"Assistant US Attorney."

"Levi Weiss is a supervising prosecutor," she said. "He manages multiple litigation in major financial and fraud cases."

"So what was he doing with something as small as Hollister?"

"I was hoping you would know."

Childers had been surprised when the case went to trial at all. He had been recovering from complications following cancer surgery at the time. Just testifying was an ordeal. He had not questioned the Government's motives in litigating.

"I was told nothing," he said. "As far as protection is concerned, you know more than I do."

"The Deputy US Marshal in charge of your detail was a woman named Valentina Flores."

"I've never heard of her, let alone talked to her."

"She's based in the DC office."

"Is that significant?"

"The Marshals Service has a large presence in the Bay area. They don't need to bring talent from DC to do protective surveillance."

"And this Flores woman qualifies as talent?"

"She's still front line enforcement," Munn said, "but the word is she's on the Service's move list."

"I have no idea what that means."

"People with potential for serial promotion in Federal law enforcement are subjected to a period of observation. The Service will rap her knuckles for the slightest faux pas to emphasize the need for political correctness. Once they are sure she has any adrenaline issues under control, they will start her up the ladder. Your assignment may have been her first rung."

"What exactly was my assignment?"

"Earl, someone has marked you for assassination."

The reality was still sinking in. It had come once before, in Vietnam. The gnawing realization that people were ready to take his life for reasons he couldn't comprehend or control.

"This is not common murder," Munn said. "The effort to get the van onto your property means someone was going to considerable trouble to disguise your death as collateral damage in a home invasion robbery. You must have some idea what it behind it."

Childers shook his head. "Can you ask your friend Tremaine?"

"Do you have any concept of who she is?"

"Just what you told me."

"She is supervising the premier Federal law enforcement agency at a major US port of entry. That is a massive responsibility. If she is handling any single case personally, it must have highly sensitive national security implications."

"Who is the Chinaman?" Childers asked.

"What?"

"You seem to know everyone. Tell me who the Chinaman is."

"Earl, what are you talking about?"

"The men who came last night were sent by someone they called the Chinaman."

Munn's professional façade was not quite enough to conceal her surprise. "The police will have to be told that."

"They know."

Childers recounted his brief talk with the police. He had been more rattled than he realized. It was an effort just to provide coherent responses to their questions. When they asked if he knew any of the intruders, he repeated the conversation he overheard as closely as he could remember it. They asked little else and he volunteered nothing.

"Have you had any dealings with China?" Munn asked.

"No."

"Chinese Nationals?"

"No."

"Anyone of Chinese descent?"

"No. None of that."

"Do you have any connection with anyone who does?"

"I'm out of the game now. Off the team. Cut from the squad. A little bird whispered in my ear that life would be easier for me if I got as far out of New York as possible."

"You were threatened?"

"Not the way you probably mean. These are finance people. Stuffed shirts. Their idea of punishment is taking you off the invitation list for next month's charity event."

"Lexie mentioned a man named Philip Linfield," Munn said. "What do you know about him?"

"Nobody knows much. Linfield is a major player in private equity. He discloses no more than he has to, which is very little."

"Could he be under FBI scrutiny?"

"I doubt it. There are very few laws to violate in private equity."

"Lexie seemed interested in his proposal for Hollister."

"People at Linfield's level play hardball, but he's lawyered up and licensed up. He has too high a profile and too big an investment in his firm to risk his reputation and his fortune in anything criminal."

Childers had needled Linfield to try to learn whether his money had come from the Middle East and might be connected with whatever had bothered Van Wyck. It was a blind shot and the fact that Linfield hadn't responded might or might not mean something.

"Where do we go from here?" Childers asked.

"I'll find out what I can. One thing you should know. Federal law enforcement agencies are not guardian angels. If they are watching over you, it is for their benefit. Not yours."

Childers' nod felt more like a shiver.

"Do not talk to the media," she said. "I'll issue a statement on your behalf. There is a formula for these situations. You're too shaken by the gravity of events to be interviewed. Gratitude to the police. Thoughts and prayers with the family of the fallen officer."

It sounded callous, but she was probably right. Nothing could bring back the officer and Childers was paying Munn for her experience and judgment.

"I'll talk to the Sheriff's people and see what they want to do about a formal interview," she said.

"Can you hold them off for a while? Same line you'll give the media. Give me a chance to stabilize."

"That's a good idea," she said, eyeing him uncertainly. "And do not under any circumstances talk to them without me present."

"Okay."

"I'm serious, Earl. Something is going on here that neither of us understands. I need to be involved."

"I get it. Message received."

Munn put her smart phone away. Childers retrieved her coat and saw her out. Afterward he sat with his eyes focused on a blank space of wall, remembering the days of coming down from combat in Vietnam and the thousand yard stare.

He had wondered then why he had remained standing while others had fallen. It certainly had nothing to do with guardian angels. His sole exposure to religion was the Presbyterian Lite thrust on him while he was growing up. Church every Sunday. Occasional social outings. A family Bible that was dusted regularly but never read. Nothing underpinning it all but an unfailing sense of responsibility and community.

Those days were gone. He was on his own now, alone in a world where people survived by their wits and initiative.

Chapter 17

VALENTINA FLORES LOST THREE HOURS flying across the country and landed at San Francisco International with a queasy stomach and a roaring hangover. She had to drag her luggage down two miles of concourse to do battle with the car rental company. Rather than waste the hike, she used her cell phone to check in with the Marshals' office.

It was Sunday morning, with junior personnel filling the duty slots. After several transfers she reached the Supervising Deputy Marshal at home. A curt briefing let her know she was Typhoid Tina. She was told to report to Lexie Tremaine. In person. Immediately. No question who was running things.

The FBI offices were buzzing when Flores arrived. Agents dressed in jeans and boots, well below Bureau standards, were checking tactical gear. Flores was escorted to Tremaine's private office.

Tremaine locked the door and lowered the blinds against slanting sun. She unlocked a closet in one corner of the room and began stripping off her street clothes, hanging each article carefully. Flores hoped she was still ripped when she reached Tremaine's age.

"Summarize the coverage of Earl Childers," Tremaine instructed.

"Two Marshal team. Vehicle mounted. Twenty four seven. Automatic weapons. Night vision equipment. No contact order remains in effect."

Tremaine removed a blue jumpsuit from a hanger and stepped into it.

"Backup?" she asked as she ran the zipper.

"County Sheriff. Ten minute response time at code two. Five minute at code three."

That had all been arranged by the local Marshals' office while Flores was enroute from DC. She had yet to talk to any of the surveillance team herself.

Tremaine took out a pair of combat boots and heavy socks and sat down to put them on.

"Air cover?" she asked.

"Rotary wing from the Sheriff's Department, assuming flyable weather. Fixed wing from the Highway Patrol. As available for surveillance. Dedicated for active situations."

Flores hoped she sounded like she knew what she was doing. Tremaine digested the information while she laced her boots. She stood and slung a blue tactical entry vest over her shoulders, velcroed it tight around her torso. The front had the standard pouches. She loaded those with her service automatic and two magazines of hollow points.

"Have you ever had a tactical situation go hot on you?"

"If you mean Marshal-involved shooting, no."

Every Deputy US Marshal knew it was possible, and no one knew until it happened to them how they would react. Flores had often tried to imagine herself in the situation, but only as a participant. Never as a supervisor. She could be looking at on-the-job training under the worst possible circumstances.

Tremaine put on a blue raid jacket with *FBI* in yellow letters on the back. "The key is to think control. Slow things down as much as possible. Buy yourself time to gather information and formulate a plan. Keep a lid on the adrenaline. Communicate your intentions clearly and don't let anyone act until they have repeated your instructions back to you."

Flores resented being lectured. She wondered whether Tremaine was emphasizing who was in charge, or just running through her own checklist for whatever she had dialed up this morning. Flores held her tongue, mindful of Webster's instructions not to get into it over anything.

Tremaine put on a blue baseball cap and locked the closet. "You do know what happened last night?"

Flores repeated what little she had been told by the Supervising Marshal. "Attempted entry at Childers' home. First responding deputy killed by gunfire. Perpetrators fled subsequent responders in a van which was later found abandoned with a deceased male inside. Center of mass gunshot. Exit wound indicated an expanding bullet or high velocity cavitation. The subject had a record. Armed robbery. Investigation is centered on oriental known associates, based on a reference to someone called the Chinaman."

"Chinaman could just be a street name," Tremaine said. "Someone who deals China white heroin."

"Does Childers have any known connection to drugs?"

"My point," Tremaine said, "is that the Sheriff's Department may be getting ahead of the evidence."

"Is there anything I should know?" Flores asked.

"My point in raising the subject," Tremaine said, "is that when one law enforcement officer is killed, every law enforcement officer feels vulnerable."

"I'll talk to my people," Flores promised, not having a clue what she would say to them.

Tremaine locked the closet and unlocked the office. "They will be jumpy for a day or two, and then they will start over-thinking situations and fail to move when they should."

"Paralysis by analysis," Flores recalled from basic training.

"There is a sweet spot in every situation. A time you can move with the best chance of success. Keep your eyes open for those."

They caught an elevator for the ride down to the garage.

"Have you had any sleep?" Tremaine asked.

"Few hours on the plane." Jet lag would hit soon.

"Have you thought about how you will contain Childers?" Tremaine asked.

"Contain him?"

"Childers is a combat veteran. If a situation arises, he may be the only one who has experienced hostile gunfire. He will react. How will you contain that reaction?"

The question was rhetorical. The elevator door opened and Tremaine went out without waiting for a response. The garage was full of agents in tactical gear, clustered around a five vehicle convoy.

"Call Oakland PD," Tremaine instructed an agent. "Advise them we are staging out now. Rendezvous point in fifteen minutes."

Flores' fifteen minutes of fame were over. If the Supervising Special Agent of a major city was personally leading a raid on Sunday, it was something gargantuan. Flores watched the convoy leave and wondered if she was missing out on something to do with Childers.

Missing out seemed to be business as usual. The Linfield bash had been a huge success. The evening had gone off flawlessly. She should be back in DC figuring out what she had done right and using it to tease an engagement ring out of Mr. William A. Montgomery III.

Instead, she was in San Fran-fucking-cisco on a babysitting job the local office should be handling. She headed the rental sedan south to check into a motel and make contact with the Childers surveillance team.

The city fell behind and she drifted into the outskirts of Silicon Valley. The streets were quiet on a Sunday. It was hard to believe the placid suburban campuses were incubators for the electronics and software that literally ran the world. Her cell phone went off to take over her life again.

"Marshal Flores," she said crisply.

"Hey, Wyatt. It's me."

"Bill. I'm sorry. I should have glanced at the caller ID."

"No worries. I just got some good news."

"So tell me."

"It's official. I just signed the paperwork for the job."

"The job?"

"Contract actually. Philip Linfield. I'll be in San Francisco as part of the advance team on the Hollister deal."

"Omigod," slipped out before she could catch it. She pulled the car into a *No Parking* zone. She was shaking too badly to drive.

"There'll be some long hours, but I thought maybe we could get together if it was convenient."

Screw convenient. It was going to happen. No matter how much finagling it took.

"Do you have a flight number and arrival time?" she asked.

"Not yet."

"Call me as soon as you get them. I'll pick you up at the airport. We'll make some plans."

"Will do," he promised. "Million things cooking right now. Gotta go."

"Love you," she said, not caring that the phone was already dead.

It had never occurred to her that Linfield would actually send people to San Francisco. She had always imagined corporate acquisitions as some pin-striped suits wheeling and dealing in a Wall Street board room. She could scarcely believe that fate had just dropped Bill into her lap. Worst case scenario, she could keep his horns trimmed down. Best case, San Francisco was a big city with no shortage of jewelry stores. She felt like climbing up on the roof of the sedan and screaming, "Woo-Hoo!" at the top of her lungs.

She put the phone away and got the car going instead. She needed to get organized. Load up on supplies. Find a good hair salon. Panic. She might have to be an arm ornament for the social side of Bill's professional life. No choice. She would have to bite the bullet, call Lexie Tremaine and find out where she bought her clothes. Screw the price. She would never get another opportunity like this. It would be full court press.

She made it about six blocks before reality set in. This was no romantic vacation. She was responsible for Earl Childers, and this time his life was in real danger. She was responsible for the Marshals guarding him. One law enforcement officer had already died, and she wasn't about to lose a Deputy US Marshal. Bill and her own life were second, but her euphoria refused to evaporate completely. At least she now had a chance to manage her opportunity with him.

Her cell went off again. This time she checked the caller ID. She didn't recognize the number.

"Marshal Flores."

"Pettinger." An unfamiliar male voice.

"Who is this?"

"Childers stakeout. We're blown."

She had met none of the Deputy Marshals she would be supervising on the assignment. Now she would be making a first impression while trying to sort out a threat she didn't understand. Tremaine's rules: Slow down. Buy Time. Gather information.

"Say again."

"Childers pulled up behind us, got out and rapped on the window. He wants you to contact him."

"Me?"

"He knew your name. First and last."

Oh, crap. Not good. She thanked the Marshal, pressed out Howard Webster's cell number. It was her turn to apologize for the timing of the call. She explained the situation.

"He asked for you by name?" Webster asked.

"He didn't get that by spotting our tail," Flores said.

"All right. Thanks, Tina. I'll pass the information up the chain."

"What do I do?"

"If Childers wants face time, give it to him. The Marshals Service has nothing to hide."

Webster's tone suggested he was as weary of the charades as she was. Childers had asked for a meeting. Maybe he knew more than he had said to the FBI. Maybe a brush with death had scared some sense into him. Maybe he would talk to her.

Chapter 18

HILIP LINFIELD'S DEPARTURE FROM HIS Connecticut compound was as hectic as a final orchestra rehearsal; the instructions for the management of his firm during an extended absence were as intricate and delicate as the most complex symphony.

Any hope that things would go more smoothly in California evaporated on arrival. It was beyond his comprehension how the limousine could be late with the total absence of traffic at three in the morning. Even San Francisco's five star Fairmont Hotel seemed asleep. It took twenty minutes to get him settled in his suite. By the time he was unpacked, the sun was rising on the business day.

Linfield's temporary offices in the city were still being furnished. He was compelled to wait for Dylan Quist in the coffee shop of the hotel where his staff would be billeted. Restaurant meetings were the stereotype of the finance industry. Linfield detested anything that made him simply part of the crowd. Circumstance had reduced him to cliché.

The venue was a sensory nightmare. Table after table of mindless chatter. Elevator music recorded by union drudges going through the motions for scale, grinding out note after note with no attention to character, nuance or purity. There was no *Wall Street Journal* in the rack. He was left with the local newspaper to take his mind off his surroundings.

The front page held nothing with national or international implications. Most of it was devoted to an FBI counter-terrorism raid in Oakland. There was a photo of a robot removing explosives from a storage unit and speculation that the raid was connected with a high-rise firebombing earlier in the month. A vicarious adrenaline jolt to keep the circulation numbers up and the advertising revenue flowing.

The business section had nothing on the Hollister acquisition. At least the information siphoned out of his organization wasn't being spread broadcast. The longer he could stay under the media's radar, the better. Linfield was reading the cultural section when Quist arrived.

"Good morning, Philip. Sorry if I'm a bit late."

Linfield lowered his paper only long enough to offer Quist a wan smile and then went back to reading.

"I was hoping to see something about one of the string ensembles San Francisco is noted for," he remarked. "Nothing dramatic. A quiet recital. Liszt, or Haydn, perhaps. Something to calm the nerves and take the edge off business."

"You might try the music department at Stanford University," Quist said. "If there's anything scheduled, they would know about it."

"An excellent suggestion," Linfield said, folding his paper and setting it aside to get on with his plan for the morning.

It was doubtful that Quist had any exposure to music beyond the groaning that emanated from the orchestra pits of over-priced theatrical productions. The question was meant to put him on notice that he was an outsider in a world he would never understand. Linfield's staff was still arriving and far from settled. It would be important to keep Quist at bay until at least some illusion of organization and control was in place.

At the same time, it was imperative to keep the project moving at full speed. There were always those with an entrenched sense of entitlement ready to foot-drag and sabotage. Anyone from fat-cat executives to feather-bedding unions could put his efforts behind schedule. The Prince would be breathing down his neck.

"I asked you to breakfast so I could keep you abreast of events," Linfield said.

"Thank you," Quist said, lifting a menu and scrutinizing the options.

It was a favorite ploy of Linfield's, and he was flattered that Quist had picked it up. It was also a chance to test the man's nerve.

"You'll be happy to know that funding for the buyout will be moving to escrow today," Linfield said, careful to hide his displeasure with the bankers and lawyers who were not willing to make it happen on a Sunday.

Quist put down the menu and raised his eyebrows. "I don't recall seeing offer documents."

"Those will be hand delivered to the board tomorrow, with the evidence of escrow deposit. I don't wish to rush anything, so I think the board meeting to vote approval should be held off until Friday."

"Held off?" Quist looked like he had swallowed his tongue.

"Just to provide time for any concerns to be addressed. Of course, if you prefer to argue for something sooner, I'll be happy to listen."

"Friday gives very little time, Philip. The documents will have to be read. Studied by counsel. Discussed with other board members."

"That," Linfield said, "is why I am giving you advance notice. So you can prepare the board members. Have them clear the decks, as it were."

"I don't know, Philip. I--"

The waitress arrived and startled Quist. She had a full complement of tables to serve and hovered impatiently. Quist took another glance at the laminated menu card and ordered an omelet and coffee.

Linfield was more particular with his diet. Cranberry juice to flush the toxins from this system. Milk and ham for protein. Whole grain cereal for carbohydrates and arterial cleansing. A plate of mixed fruit. His mind and body were heat engines, and his focus and performance would be only as good as the fuel he took in. He resumed control of the conversation as soon as the server was gone.

"The shareholders will receive the offer and voting instructions next Monday. I would like to have board approval in place this Friday afternoon, so their recommendation can be transmitted with the notification."

"Correct me if I am wrong, Philip, but aren't there a considerable number of filings to be made prior to the buyout?"

"In progress as we speak," Linfield assured him.

"And there is approval from the government."

Linfield hadn't liked circulating his plans in Government circles, even on a limited basis, but his lobbying firm had insisted. They needed advance notice to build support among Members of Congress and bureaucrats for a venture this size. Quist seemed even less comfortable than he was.

"I've been notified that I will be interviewed by the Department of Treasury."

"As will I," Linfield said.

"I know virtually nothing about the transaction," Quist protested. "What will I tell them?"

"If you don't know, tell them you don't know. There is no substitute for the truth."

"I'm not sure why you are in such a hurry," Quist said.

Confiding in the fellow was out of the question. Even without specific mention of The Prince. Just the knowledge that Linfield was under pressure would play to Quist's advantage. Better to summon generic demons to hurry him along.

"Competition, Dylan. Every day we delay our move into the market gives the competition one more day to catch up with our technology. I would hope that as CEO you would understand the critical importance of market share."

"Of course."

Quist's nerves were visible in his features, but Linfield knew the argument was growing redundant. It would be less effective with each repetition. Even now Quist was wavering.

"I'm just not sure I can recommend acceptance on such short notice," Quist said.

At least the lack of specific objections was good news. Quist was scrambling for answers. The trick now was to keep him back on his heels. Linfield offered an encouraging smile.

"As I understand, Dylan, given your current ownership position in Hollister and based on current market price, you will receive nearly one million dollars for the vested portion of the shares you were granted when you took over as CEO and garnered in subsequent bonus awards."

Quist did not smile. "Forty percent of the initial grant is not yet vested. The situation is worse for subsequent annual grants."

Linfield knew Quist's financial situation at least as well as Quist did. Hollister's controller had been identified early in the evaluation process as a potential contact inside the firm. A Philippine national. Short tenure. An ambitious woman isolated in a male culture. She had provided a detailed breakout of Quist's stock grants on date of hire and annual bonus grants since then.

The grants were on a five year vesting schedule, meant to keep Quist in place over time. He took ownership of twenty percent of each grant every year he remained with Hollister. He would leave well more than a million dollars in unvested grants on the table. Not an appetizing proposition in an environment where CEOs routinely received seven figure annual compensation.

"And some of the vesting is recent," Quist protested, "which will disqualify any income from favorable capital gains tax treatment."

"The timing is perhaps not ideal," Linfield conceded, "however you might be well to temper your analysis with some situational awareness. If the acquisition does not take place, share price could suffer dramatically. You might well be better off surrendering fewer shares at a high price than a larger number in a fire sale. Even net of tax considerations."

"I'm not opposing the acquisition, per se," Quist was quick to assure him. "I merely think a little consultation may be in order before we move. Make sure everyone is on board. That sort of thing."

Quist's answer gave Linfield the information he was seeking. The fellow had done the arithmetic and knew precisely what he would net from a sale. And what he would lose as a result of the majority of his share grants not having enough time to vest and mature as capital gains. A delay of only months could net him several hundred thousand dollars. Linfield would need to contact the largest shareholders directly to ensure that Quist didn't stall things for his own benefit.

Linfield understood Quist; a man not unlike himself, albeit cast from a cruder mold and arrogant beyond his capabilities. His attitude toward control transcended desire and wandered into the addictive realm of compulsion. As his fingers were pried one by one from the levers of power he would grow increasingly uncomfortable, until he finally left of his own accord, clinging all the while to the fantasy that Hollister was doomed without his unerring vision and paternal guidance.

The wild card was Earl Childers. If anything, the fellow had an aversion to control. His background suggested a man content to drift, taking whatever fate offered and making what he could of it. Circumstances had left him in a position where he might fatally delay Linfield's plans. He would have to be sounded out to determine his position on the immediacy of the transaction.

Chapter 19

$\mathcal{E}$ ARL CHILDERS WAS NOT EXPECTING anyone when the door chimes rang early Monday morning. The caller was a woman in her late twenties, rangy and athletic. Black hair curled inward at her jaw, framing features that suggested Imperial Spain had mingled with Native America somewhere in her ancestry. Even in slacks and a fashionable leather jacket she looked, in the drifting Northern California fog, like a primordial huntress stalking back through the mists of time. She smiled and opened a leather identification wallet.

"Deputy US Marshal Valentina Flores, Mr. Childers. You asked to see me?"

Flores' voice was pleasant, without the overtone of authority he had expected from the hard-charging Federal careerist Doreen Munn had described.

"Thank you for coming," he said.

He ushered her into the living room, installed her on the sofa and, when she declined coffee, sat in a chair facing her.

"I understand you--meaning the Marshals Service--have me under surveillance as a protective measure."

"Where did you get that information?" Flores asked.

In fact Childers had only seen a sedan with Federal license plates remain after the Sheriff's investigators had left and guessed that the Marshals Service was back.

"Isn't it public knowledge?"

Flores' smile flickered, as if she regretted opening the subject. "What did you want to talk about?"

"Is there was anything I should be doing to help?" he asked. "Set you up for success?"

"Do you have any idea who might want to harm you?"

"I was hoping you knew what the threat was."

"You testified for the Prosecution in a Federal criminal trial."

A trial that normally wouldn't have happened, prosecuted by a man too highly placed to be personally involved in litigation. The trial was not what it seemed to be. Something more than simple fraud was involved. Something Childers had not been told about.

"Some months ago," he said.

"Have you received any threats?"

The two attempts on his life had come out of the blue. The first involved a man he barely knew, just returned from the Middle-East and agitated about something to do with Hollister. The second was apparently commissioned by someone called the Chinaman.

"No," was all he told Flores.

"Did your trial testimony concern a firm named Hollister?" Flores asked.

"Yes." That was public knowledge, and he was surprised she wasn't aware of it.

"Is there any unusual activity at Hollister?" she asked.

"The firm is expecting a buyout offer."

"Is there anything unusual about the offer?"

"I don't know. It hasn't been tendered."

She was the second Federal Agent interested in Hollister, but who didn't pursue the subject. She asked questions about the alarm system, warned him not to carry or try to use any personal weapons and went through a list of security precautions.

"Here is my business card. It has my cell number and e-mail address. If you can provide your daily itinerary, that will be helpful."

"Certainly."

"Keep your cell phone with you. Keep it turned on at all times."

"All right."

"Do not contact the Marshals on the surveillance, or tell anyone they are there. In the event of an emergency, follow their instructions."

They toured the interior and exterior of the house. She thanked him for his time and left with his day's itinerary; a session at the health club, a trip to the supermarket and a meeting with a contractor to get a bid on repairing his gate.

Rain began while he was talking to the contractor, a harbinger of one of the storms that seemed to blow in frequently off the Pacific. The phone was ringing when he went in to shed his wet hoodie.

"Pilar Monterosa, Mr. Childers. From Hollister. You asked me to let you know if I received any information about the Linfield proposal."

"Yes."

"It might be better if we talked privately. Would it be all right if I came to your home?"

"Certainly," Childers said.

"It will have to be in the evening. After work. Will eight be suitable?"

"I'll be expecting you," Childers said.

Her voice lingered in his mind after she hung up. He cursed himself for a fool, but that didn't stop him vacuuming, straightening furniture and cleaning the kitchen immediately after dinner.

The door chimes rang promptly at eight.

The rain had grown to a steady downpour, slanted by a wind that brought furtive noises from the nearby shrubbery. Pilar stood close in the shelter of the alcove. She wore an evening coat with the collar turned against the storm and fur caressing her cheeks. The porch lamps raised highlights in a black Jaguar coupe in the driveway behind her. Until now, Childers had seen her only in business environments, and only as attractive, never elegant. Her fragrance filled his nostrils as she stepped quickly into the sanctuary of the entry. He closed out the rain and the cold and the two of them were alone, isolated by the night and the weather.

She unslung her shoulder bag to allow him to help her out of the coat. The dress beneath was cut to flatter a slim figure, emphasizing without revealing. Childers hung the coat carefully in the entry closet, escorted her into the living room.

"Would you like something to drink?"

"I brought my own tea," she said. "I hope that is all right?"

Tea wasn't something Childers was accustomed to making. He was reduced to allowing Pilar to forage through the kitchen cupboards to locate a kettle and pot. While the tea was steeping she let her gaze wander. Half a level down and open to the kitchen was the recreation room. Something there caught her eye.

"Oh, you have Uncle Scrooge."

The picture was a framed cel of the Disney cartoon character Scrooge McDuck. Bought originally because it took Childers back to a youth of haunting comic book racks, it hung now in a room notable for a pool table and an old Rock-Ola Jukebox, memories from an Officers' Club stag bar at his first Army posting. He had furnished the room as a refuge, a passport to innocent times and events frozen in history. With an attractive younger woman in the house, it was a reminder that he was just one more old man bundled in a cardigan to ward off the chill of passing years. He turned on the lights for her.

She descended the stairs and stood almost reverently before the picture of a white-whiskered old duck who existed only in the imagination.

"I saw the magazine this came from," she decided. "A reprint, I think. Many years ago, when I was quite small and full of dreams."

Childers had seen Pilar only in the moment, never as someone with a past. Someone like himself, with a childhood, with dreams. He wondered what those dreams might have been but he dared not ask. He was already intruding on her personal time, and if she were willing to share, fairness would open his own life to questions for which he had no reasonable answers. He held his tongue until she was ready to return to the kitchen.

Pilar poured tea for herself. Childers declined in favor of soda. It was a way of maintaining distance appropriate to his age and the fact that she had come on business. They went back to the living room. She took a laptop from her shoulder bag and opened it on the coffee table where they could both see the screen if they sat close to one another on the sofa.

"These are the numbers that came in today regarding the buyout proposal," she said.

He watched her bring them up, unsettled by the warmth of her nearness and careful to focus his attention on the display.

"How widely are these known?" Childers asked.

"They will go to the board as official notification tomorrow. A courier should bring you a copy."

Childers scanned the figures as Pilar scrolled down the spreadsheet. He was aware that she was watching his eyes. Perhaps just to see how fast she should scroll. More likely to gauge his reaction. A quick calculation told him how much he would receive from the purchase of his shares. Pilar had already done the numbers.

"You should do well," she said and then hesitated, studying his face, "although perhaps not as well as if money could have been raised through capitalization or borrowing in lieu of buyout."

"I don't think that was ever in the cards," Childers said.

For the owners it was a choice of cashing out immediately on Linfield's terms or risking a steady decline in share price. Employees like Pilar would have to make their own peace with the new order.

"Then you plan to vote for approval?" she asked.

"Barring any issues in the actual offer documents," Childers said.

"Do you require anything else?" she asked.

"No. Thank you so much for coming. I'm sorry to bring you out on so nasty a night."

She powered down the laptop and closed it. "You are fortunate to have such a nice home."

"And such nice company," he said. "I wish our evening didn't have to end."

He regretted the statement as soon as he made it. It was juvenile and embarrassing.

Pilar smiled. "It doesn't have to."

*   *

Pilar had to leave for work early the next morning. The phone rang as her Jaguar was pulling away.

"Ray Parker, Earl. Did I get you out of bed?"

"No. Did you find something?"

"I had breakfast with Miss Tenacity from the *Journal.* They came up with a probable for Linfield's insider."

"They've been working on it all this time?"

"That's what I've been trying to tell you, Earl. Too much horsepower for a small feature."

"Who is their candidate?"

"Pilar Monterosa. You know who she is?"

"Hollister's controller." Childers sat down.

"Born in the Philippines. Grew up in an orphanage in a place called Quezon City, just outside Manila. Got a job in the branch of a British bank. She must have impressed them big time. They brought her to the home office and finagled her some classes at the London School of Economics. She aced them all. On the fast track to a top job when the recession hit. Superstars started dropping like flies. Next thing anyone knows, she's head bean counter at an oil drilling service company. No one knows how she got the job, how she got a visa or why she's wasting her time there."

"Not likely," Childers decided.

"You think they're jiving me?" Parker asked.

"When it comes to billions, Linfield is single digits. British banks play in hundreds of billions. She must have made contacts while she was there."

"Maybe she couldn't score?"

"The outfit is Chanel. The pearls are Mikimoto. She's got it and she knows how to use it."

"Earl, has this broad got her legs wrapped around you?"

"Not at the moment."

"Come on, Earl. You didn't just fall off a produce truck. You know how this shit works. You start out thinking wham-bam-thank-you-ma'am. Before you know it, you're in over your head."

"Why would she waste it on me?"

"Earl, this is a first class mind travelling on a third world passport. A marriage license is a lot more security than a work permit."

"Forget it, Ray. Drop the whole thing."

"So what do I tell the *Journal?*"

"Ray, two people were shot dead outside my home night before last."

"Jesus Fucking Christ. What did Van Wyck get onto in the Middle East?"

"Just bail out."

Childers cradled the phone. Counting collateral damage from the Savannah bombing, fourteen people were dead. People he didn't know were trying to kill him. Now he was receiving attention from a woman with no visible reason to be involved with him or Hollister. The possibility was growing that Linfield's offer concealed something bigger, and probably darker, than just the man and his organization.

Childers was ill-prepared to meet the challenge. He dared not call on any remaining contacts he might have for fear of endangering them. All he could do was see a doctor about the fatigue that continued to dog him.

Chapter 20

VALENTINA FLORES HAD CLEARED THE decks for a whirlwind when Bill arrived. She arrived at the airport with a head full of plans and wound up driving the light of her life, two of his co-workers and a trunk full of luggage to a downtown hotel. Tonight's dinner in Union Square was the first time she had seen him since. The poor guy had aged three years in the last three days.

"Are my eyes really bloodshot?" he asked.

"Seriously, Bill, how much sleep have you had?"

"Tina, this assignment is the finance guy's equivalent of catching the world's most wanted terrorist. Even if I don't land a permanent position with Linfield, I'll gain five years worth of experience in five weeks. And I'll finally have something solid in my resume."

"Just don't kill yourself. Okay?"

"Hey, you're not the only tough cookie on the planet, you know."

Her smile felt feeble.

"Tell you what," he said. "I should have Sunday open. Why don't you pull together a list of the sights you want to see? We'll make a day of it. Just the two of us."

A fast kiss and a hug, an agreement to meet Sunday morning and Bill was gone back to his career. She wondered if she had suddenly become the center of his love life because he saw her as a connection to this Hollister opportunity. She shouldn't complain. High school romance was a long time ago, and she hadn't scored that well even then.

So what if Bill did see her as something to boost his career? At least that gave her a foot in the door. A shot at turning his head around.

Those were her competitive juices flowing. The same knee-jerk reaction that had brought her to this point in her life. She had won dance contests. A shelf full of trophies waiting to be shined. She had fought her way through college. A line on her resume. She had beaten out a shitload of candidates for a Deputy Marshals' slot. Now she was on a merry-go-round assignment no one seemed to understand. Suppose she managed to maneuver Bill down the aisle? Would they wind up two strangers staring at each other across the breakfast table? Her cell phone jolted her back to reality.

"Marshal Flores."

"Tremaine. How soon can you get into the city?" She sounded on edge, not the cool supervisor Flores had seen in the past.

"I'm in the city," Flores said.

"I need surveillance," Tremaine said. "I can't send an FBI agent, and I can't explain why."

Accepting orders directly from an FBI supervisor would be a violation of Marshals Service protocol, but Webster had told her Tremaine was running things in San Francisco.

"This will be an auto tail," Tremaine said. "Female subject. Black Jaguar coupe."

Flores found the license number in her phone memory. This was Pilar Monterosa. Earl Childers' honey. One surveillance shift had logged her into Childers' home at eight in the evening. The next shift logged her out at seven thirty the next morning. Inquiries established that she was a corporate officer at Hollister.

Something was wrong at that company. Maybe following the Monterosa woman would give her some clue what it was. Nothing else had.

Tremaine provided a call-back number. "There should be no issues, but if trouble develops, back off. There can be no tactical callout on this."

More mystery.

"On my way," Flores said.

She got a taste of the old feeling. Not quite the adrenaline rush of closing in on a wanted felon, but more action than she had seen in some time. The address Tremaine had given her was a high-rise condo. Circling the block was pointless. There was no such thing as an empty parking space in San Francisco. She pulled into a bus zone on a side street, pointed toward the exit from the tower's underground garage, and settled to wait.

The last vestiges of twilight faded into the steady glow of street lamps. Traffic dwindled to few passing cars. Autumn chill and a brisk wind kept the sidewalks all but clear of pedestrians.

Eventually a black Jaguar nosed out of the tower's garage. The driver was alone. She sat with a petite woman's habitual erectness and looked left and right with more caution than the sparse traffic warranted. Flores gave her a block lead.

A maroon Escalade fell in half a block behind Monterosa's Jaguar. The passengers appeared to be a man and a woman of no more than medium stature. The Cadillac was ostentatious for surveillance, but not out of place on high-end urban street. Nothing about it was suspicious or threatening. Flores waited through several turns. When she was sure its presence behind the Jaguar wasn't just a coincidence, she used her cell phone.

"Tremaine."

"Flores. I'm not the only tail your subject has." She described the Cadillac, gave the license number. "Subject just turned off Embarcadero. Looks like she wants to go south on the Bay Bridge Freeway."

"Has your surveillance been compromised?"

"No."

"All right. Thank you."

Tremaine was gone, leaving Flores no clue what she should do if the Cadillac became a threat. Flores followed the Escalade onto the freeway ramp and checked the side mirror to merge into traffic.

Her heart jumped into her throat. Headlights were bearing down on her at extreme speed. She hugged the right lane and pulled her shoulder bag close to have ready access to her service automatic.

A Dodge Charger shot past at well over a hundred miles an hour, pulled in behind the Escalade ahead and spread blue and red strobe light all over the highway. Flores' heart rate subsided. The Escalade pulled over. Flores went past in the normal flow of traffic.

One call to Tremaine and the Highway Patrol picked those jokers off in nothing flat. The coverage must have been prearranged. Best guess: The trooper would ID the occupants of the Escalade, issue a warning for some trumped up civil violation and send them on their way none the wiser that they'd been busted. That would free the Monterosa woman to do whatever she planned.

Monterosa's Jaguar doubled back across the bridge and exited the freeway. What followed was a twisting climb up surface streets, a dizzying drop down Market, a left on Stockton and then another climb up California. This was the most vertical city Flores had ever seen. Monterosa's route proved to be the long way around to the Mark Hopkins Hotel. Flores had heard of the place and promised herself a look, but this wasn't quite what she had planned.

Monterosa turned the Jaguar over to a valet. Flash ride. Curb service. Five star digs. Nothing but the best for this babe. Flores pulled past, parked on the drop off loop and got out.

A valet loped up. "Ma'am, you can't park--"

"US Marshals Service." Flores showed her badge, and gave him a smile for insurance. "Leave it where it is, please."

"Yes, ma'am."

A high-heeled trot got Flores into the lobby not far behind the Monterosa woman. Her quarry was crossing toward the elevator bank. The woman's pace was demure and an overcoat smothered any curves she had, but she still drew surreptitious glances from more than a few men. Flores wasn't plugged into male thinking, but she knew heat when she saw it in action. This chick came from where they made it.

Flores cringed at the thought of Bill winding up in the same room with her. The same building would be bad enough. Flores hoped Childers had the woman on a short leash. They made an odd couple. Based on her visit, Flores read Childers as smart and cagey, defensive rather than conspiratorial. Not the kind of man to romance a hottie more than thirty years his junior, or turn up as the subject of an FBI profile. His role in whatever was going on and the full extent of his relationship with the Monterosa woman were a cipher.

Monterosa boarded an elevator. Flores had to risk riding up with her. At least dinner with Bill had left her dressed for the trip. They were alone in the car and Flores decided eye contact and a quick smile would be the least suspicious tack.

Monterosa's return smile was reserved, with a startling hint of vulnerability. Her coat had cost as much as Flores' rent. She had cheekbones to die for. Her fragrance was a floral exotic that probably translated to something like *Dream But Don't Touch*. Still, she didn't seem entirely sure of herself. At least not in the company of another woman.

They rode to nineteen and disembarked. Monterosa paused at the entrance to the *Top of the Mark*. After a glance inside, she sprung for the five dollar cover. Flores paid and went in after her. It would be worth the money for a look at the guy who could persuade this honey to go Dutch treat in San Francisco's most romantic night spot.

The place was all it was advertised to be. Club ambience, sultry jazz and a stunning three-sixty view of the night lit city. It was definitely going on her list of must-drag-Bill-to locations.

Monterosa was already seated on a couch by a window. The man with her was trying for an upscale Don Juan look in a sport coat and an open collar shirt. It wasn't working. He was tall, tanned, muscular. Short hair and a clean shave gave him an aura of commando chic. Monterosa hadn't bothered unbuttoning her overcoat, let alone taking it off. Apparently love was not in the air. Flores helped herself to a nearby chair and began glancing at the door, hoping to give the impression that Mister-Right-For-Tonight was pushing his luck if he didn't show soon.

Monterosa and the man on the couch were only a few feet away. Rather than keeping their voices low, they spoke in Spanish. Nice try, folks. Tina cut her baby teeth on Espanol.

The meeting was over in fifteen minutes and Flores left as Monterosa was collecting her shoulder bag, staying ahead of her in case the man was watching to see if anyone followed. She caught her own elevator going down. Outside she started her sedan and waited for the valet to bring Monterosa's Jaguar.

A quick trip back to the condo and Monterosa was inside again. Flores called Tremaine and gave her a thumbnail sketch of events.

"Your subject has a distinct Philippine accent," Flores said. "The man got his Spanish from *Rosetta Stone*."

"How do you know?"

"Speech patterns. Response time. She could think in Spanish. He had to mentally translate to whatever his native language was. Probably English, from the way he butchered the inflections."

"What did they talk about?"

"Something they called an insertion. She said she didn't have a date, but it would occur at Fort Apache."

"What did the man say?"

"Mostly questions. How many would be involved. What sort of equipment. She thought about a dozen, but had no details."

"Anything else?"

"His body language gave me the impression that he wanted to make a personal move on her, but either he wasn't sure how or he couldn't get up the nerve."

"Thank you," Tremaine said. "None of this happened."

"Yes, Ma'am," Flores said into a dead phone.

Tremaine hadn't asked for a description of the man, so she must have known who he was. Ditto the terms insertion and Fort Apache, neither of which meant anything to Flores. Tremaine had probably also known the conversation would be in Spanish, and knew from Flores' Service bio that she was bilingual. Whatever the case, Tremaine was running things and she didn't have to tell anyone shit. None of which explained why Tremaine couldn't send an FBI team tonight.

Flores decided she should be grateful she had been picked for the surveillance. Without it, she would have been blind to the shadow play behind her assignment. And maybe that was the point. Maybe Tremaine was trying to keep her in the loop. At least now she had a better idea where to look for trouble.

Chapter 21

PHILIP LINFIELD BEGAN THE SAN Francisco phase of the Hollister acquisition to the strains of Mozart; music that filled him with energy and sharpened his focus. The early results were gratifying. The Monterosa woman was right about Childers' inclination to recommend approval. Perhaps she had thought it within her charter to provide a little nudge. While Linfield didn't encourage that sort of thing, neither did he discourage individual initiative when it came to earning the incentives available in connection with the successful conclusion of his projects. The shareholders were the usual flock of sheep. The margin of acceptance had been overwhelming.

Beyond acceptance lay they inevitable tangle of regulations. Weeks of tedious labor. Conferences and filings. Dotting i's. Crossing t's. The Prince's functionaries nagged constantly for progress reports. The tempo of events grew as frenetic as a jazz run, until Linfield finally had the end in sight.

The only remaining hurdle was Treasury Department approval. Linfield's cell phone rang while he was selecting a suit for his interview. The caller ID caught his attention.

"Hello, Elmer. I was hoping to hear from you long before now. I did mention the urgent nature of plugging the information leaks."

"Philip, it's one thing to locate an actual person. It's quite another to establish that no such person exists."

"Elmer, what are you ranting about?"

"The name you gave me is a fictitious identity created for an FBI undercover specialist currently assigned to a counter-terrorism task force."

"Good Lord." Linfield sank into a chair.

"And the woman you mentioned as his dance partner…"

"Flores? Was that her name?"

"Valentina Flores. Deputy United States Marshal."

"Elmer, I depend on you to remain in daily contact with our friends in the Administration. I expect to be informed, in advance, when any of my transactions are expected to come under hostile scrutiny."

"This is not an inquiry into financial irregularities, Philip. And it is not small. The FBI and the Marshals Service have been fighting turf battles ever since J. Edgar Hoover finagled powers of arrest for his people back in the day. The only authority that can force them to cooperate is the Department of Homeland Security."

The Prince's penchant for Islamist bombast came immediately to mind. The fellow had received the finest education his family's oil riches could provide, and now his buffoonery threatened to spook Homeland Security and turn Linfield's exquisitely orchestrated financial symphony into a Gilbert and Sullivan farce.

"Elmer, I need a no nonsense assessment. Right now. Is there an identifiable threat to the Hollister acquisition?"

"The Flores woman is in San Francisco."

"Doing what?"

"Her assignment is witness protection for a man named Earl Childers."

Childers might have realized his single seat on the board wouldn't give him enough clout to kill the Hollister deal, feigned cooperation and slunk off to the Government with some tale of Muslim bogey men.

"Is the Treasury Department involved?" Linfield asked.

"Treasury requested the protection following the first attempt on Childers' life."

"Attempt on his life?"

"There have been two," Elmer said. "You were not aware of that?"

"No."

"Philip, I don't want to sound alarmist, but the level and nature of Government involvement suggests there may be some physical threat involved here."

"I can't use speculation," Linfield said. "I need facts. Find out what is going on and get back to me. And Elmer, sooner rather than later."

The taxi ride to the Federal Building gave Linfield time to stew. Before Elmer's call, all the pieces of the Hollister acquisition seemed to be in place. The spade work had been done. The contacts made. The campaign contributions tendered. No concerns had arisen. Now, at the last possible second, he learned there were potentially significant facts at large. He would be going into a critical interview groping through a fog of uncertainty. Postponement was not an option. The Prince's deadline had already passed. Linfield paid the driver and chafed through lobby security.

Insipid elevator music put an edge on his already taut nerves. A receptionist deposited him in a small conference room, an interior space without windows, the walls plain, the whiteboard carelessly erased. Lack of electronics would limit the meeting to only those present. It was a surprise that the interview was being conducted in San Francisco. Linfield's legal staff had anticipated a trip to DC. Until now, Linfield had taken the venue to mean the Hollister acquisition was low on Treasury's radar and the interview would be part of a rubber-stamping process. After Elmer's call, he wondered if Treasury had already decided to scuttle the deal and weren't going to waste any effort on pleasantries. The door opened and Linfield stood to greet two men.

"Roland Ohashi," the younger announced. "US Department of Treasury."

He was thirty-something, unsmiling. If he ran true to type, he would be hoping to use his government posting as a springboard to a lucrative position in private industry. Linfield's success had earned him a full share of envy. Any of his competitors would gladly reward someone who derailed his plans.

The older man offered a hand. "Levi Weiss, Mr. Linfield. Attorney General's Office."

Weiss had the unassuming manner often cultivated by highly placed Government officials. A senior representative of the Justice Department was both unexpected and unwelcome. Linfield had taken a gamble in not bringing his own attorney. Lawyers wrangling over legal trivia could slow the process when he needed to expedite. For better or worse, he was committed.

The three of them sat down.

Ohashi opened a briefcase. He took his time getting situated, amateurish and unnecessary notice that the interview would proceed at his pace.

"The subject of this meeting," he said for the benefit of a recorder, "is the examination of the proposed private purchase and de-listing of Hollister, Inc., a publicly traded US firm."

He mispronounced the name of the purchasing firm and demanded proof that Linfield had authority to act on their behalf. Linfield presented a sheet of vellum letterhead naming him agent of record for the firm, over the signature of a Swiss attorney.

Ohashi scowled at the letter and passed it to Weiss for inspection. Even as theatre it was ludicrous. Neither had any way to know whether the document was a forgery, or an outright fraud. Ohashi consigned it to a folder.

"According to documents filed with the Treasury Department," Ohashi said, "you are proposing the buyout of Hollister by a foreign domiciled firm."

"The firm," Linfield said, "is duly licensed in the United States and is current on all taxes and fees."

"You do understand, Mr. Linfield, that you are proposing placing a participant in the key industrial sector of petroleum recovery under foreign control?"

This twit had some nerve, after Treasury had mortgaged the entire country to the Communist government of China to pay for ill-managed social programs and out-of-control military adventures, to imply that Linfield was disloyal.

"The purpose of the transaction," Linfield said, projecting as much calm as he could, "is to enable Hollister to compete in the global industrial control systems market. Currently the United States has defaulted this activity to foreign firms, some of which enjoy massive government subsidies to tilt the playing field to their advantage."

"You are proposing the sale of Hollister to a foreign firm," Ohashi pointed out.

"This transaction will not move any of Hollister's facilities or jobs off shore," Linfield said. "It will bring both favorable trade and significant new employment to the country. In short, it will enhance economic, and by extension national, security rather than degrade it."

The Prince's role was purely financial. He was an investor. He would receive a fair return and nothing more. Linfield had no intention of surrendering even the appearance of operational control to him.

"Based on an earlier interview," Ohashi said with the exaggerated innocence trial lawyers were fond of feigning, "Hollister's current management seems singularly uninformed as to these plans."

"Hollister's current management," Linfield replied, "is the financial steward for the incumbent shareholders of record. It is neither privy to the plans nor subject to the instructions of the proposed owner."

"Do you envision replacing the current management?"

"Not en bloc," Linfield said.

Quist had probably put forth a final, feeble effort to sabotage the project by raising the specter of a horde of foreigners descending on Hollister's executive suite. The fellow had only hastened his own departure.

"Of course," Linfield added, "all staffing is subject to ongoing review, and individuals may, of their own volition, elect to pursue other opportunities."

"We will need a summary of the changes you intend to make in Hollister's operations," Ohashi said.

"Past is prologue," Linfield said. "Contemplated modifications are entirely in scope and scale; to broaden product capabilities and to cultivate a national and international customer base."

"Treasury will need specifics," Ohashi insisted.

Linfield couldn't afford to put the details of his business plan in the public domain. His competitors would make a meal of the information.

"We have received no written request for such material," he said.

"This is not a request!"

The petulant outburst caught Linfield by surprise. Ohashi was acting like a child who had a toy snatched away. Linfield wondered how much control he had over the interview and how much had been scripted for him. Weiss showed smoker's teeth in a conciliatory smile.

"Mr. Linfield, Mr. Ohashi is simply trying to meet his due diligence requirements."

"I have responded to the best of my ability," Linfield said.

Ohashi had to be content with scribbling a note and moving on.

It was becoming clear that this interview was pro-forma. Someone in government had decided that the Hollister acquisition would go forward. They had shunted the venue to the west coast and sent a junior staffer to look after the requisite details. Ohashi resented the role of errand boy. Weiss had been sent as a monitor, to make sure everything went as planned.

What the plan was Linfield couldn't begin to guess. The fact that both the project and his firm were under Government scrutiny was disturbing, but he had a significant investment of time, money and reputation in the Hollister acquisition. At this point all he could do was accept the victory he was being handed, let the meeting drone on to its conclusion and defer other questions, no matter how serious they might be.

Chapter 22

*O*N THE MORNING FOLLOWING THE Hollister buyout, Earl Childers logged onto his bank's customer service website to reconcile the overnight deposit against the market value of the shares he surrendered. The door chimes broke his concentration.

The caller was a woman around fifty. Childers did not recognize her, beyond noting that her overcoat and grooming suggested East Coat money rather than the more casual style that prevailed locally.

"Earl Childers?" she inquired in a clipped, aristocratic soprano.

"Yes."

"My name is Catherine Van Wyck. I have come a long way to see you. I would appreciate a few minutes of your time."

Her heels clicked on the entry parquet. She shed her coat and handed it to him to hang in the closet, as if he were domestic help. Her gaze was direct, not the look of someone who expected refreshment or social niceties. She sat unbidden on the sofa, the effects of regular gym visits obvious under a pencil skirt and loose top, and waited until Childers seated himself.

"My husband came to San Francisco to see you just before he was killed. I would like to know what the two of you talked about."

"He invited me to a meeting," Childers said.

"Nothing more?" Skeptical eyes scolded him.

"Your husband was quite taken with the concept of social stratification. He--"

"He was a snob," she said. "So am I. There is no point dwelling on trivial shortcomings."

No tears. No illusions. This was no grieving widow, and there was nothing to be gained treating her like one.

"The point, Mrs. Van Wyck, is that this conversation is on the fast track to nowhere. Your husband didn't confide in me. I expect because he saw me as no more than a pawn in whatever he was doing. Had I gone to the meeting, I might have learned what he wanted. I certainly would now be too dead to tell you about it. If you have come to interrogate me, you have wasted a trip. If you wish to share what he told you, we might be able to pool our knowledge."

She had a high, tinkling laugh, like a wine glass shattering. "My but you are blunt, aren't you?"

"Mrs. Van Wyck, I didn't ask your husband to come and see me."

"And what exactly is this knowledge you expect to pool?"

"Your husband must have said something to you."

"Spenser and I indulged in marriage because it was and remains the socially and legally accepted form of intimate companionship. We would have been together without it but we were not soul mates, or whatever the common psychobabble is. There were things I did not tell him because our partnership was better off for his ignorance. There were things he did not tell me, I suspect out of some protective sense of chivalry."

"What was the last thing he said before he left? Do you remember?"

"Verbatim."

"Can you share it, along with the circumstances?"

"He was going out the door to catch the airport shuttle, and he said, 'You know, Cat, these morons in Government have gone as far as to admit the next Pearl Harbor will be electronic, but they won't do thing one to stop it'. He pecked me on the cheek and left."

"Did you report that to the FBI when they interviewed you?"

"How did you know they interviewed me?" she demanded.

"If they talked to me, they certainly talked to you. And probably told you not to discuss the interview."

"Yes."

"How did your husband come to use that particular condominium unit?"

"It belonged to friends of my family who are out of the country. Spenser called and asked if I could get him permission to use it. He said he needed it for a meeting. He was quite mysterious beyond that."

"That," Childers realized, "gave whoever killed your husband and the others a very narrow window of time to build the bomb."

"Yes, it did."

"And leaves only a short list of people who knew where and when to detonate it," he added.

"Yes."

As the sole absentee at the meeting, Childers should have been the logical suspect.

"Did you know any of the people killed with our husband?" he asked.

"That is one of the questions I came three thousand miles to ask you."

"Ask what you came to ask, Mrs. Van Wyck. I will do my best, but I will make no apologies for inadequacy."

"I've seen a lot of inadequacy in the last few days, Mr. Childers, and had no apologies. What is Hollister?"

"A firm providing logistical services to the petroleum recovery industry."

"Nothing electronic?" she asked.

"They have developed a computerized industrial control system for off-shore drilling platforms."

"Could that have been what Spenser was talking about?"

"There is only a single installation on a small platform. Anyone who wanted to turn off-shore drilling into something as catastrophic as Pearl Harbor would target one or more of the platforms in the Gulf of Mexico. Some are as large as a small city, and their software is older and more vulnerable."

"Spenser was quite insistent about talking to someone in authority at Hollister," she said. "Is there anything unusual going on there?"

"The firm was just bought out."

"That doesn't happen every day."

"It was a normal business transaction done under Government scrutiny. Since the purchaser was foreign domiciled, the bar was even higher."

"Foreign?" she asked sharply.

"Swiss registered. That's a common tax haven."

"Spenser was told something on his visit to the middle east," she insisted.

"What was he doing there?"

"Do you know what SWOT analysis is?"

SWOT was a business acronym for Strengths, Weaknesses, Opportunities and Threats.

"Anything specific?" Childers asked.

"The Middle East is full of competing sects, tribes and families, each trying to frustrate the others' ambitions. Spenser has contacts all over. He spent his trips picking up various bits of tittle-tattle. Anything that might allow the bank to get a foot in the door or keep them out of trouble. Something he heard last time terrified him."

"Do you know Philip Linfield?" Childers asked.

"I know of him. Married above his station. Spent the last twenty odd years trying to become something other than nouveau riche."

"He brokered the buyout," Childers said. "He didn't reply when I asked if his money was sourced from the Middle East."

"Didn't reply?"

"It may mean nothing," he said. "It struck me as odd only because he had a response to everything else."

Catherine Van Wyck stood, smiling for the first time since she had come. "Thank you for your time, Mr. Childers. I hope my visit hasn't been an inconvenience."

Childers stood. "I don't mean to be dramatic, Mrs. Van Wyck, but whatever is going on has killed fourteen people."

"The time since my husband's death, Mr. Childers, has been spent, among other things, fending off no end of ludicrous alpha-males who seem to think I should be looking for a pair of broad shoulders to protect me from the vicissitudes of life. Spenser was not perfect, as a man or a partner, but he was what I had and I am not simply going to sniffle at his memorial service and go hide under the bed. Whoever is responsible for his death will pay."

"As you wish, Mrs. Van Wyck."

"One more question," she said. "Why didn't you go to the meeting when Spenser asked? Did you and your ilk really despise him that much?"

"My ilk?"

"Closet whiners. Legends in your own minds. Bitter because fate dealt you a life of following orders rather than giving them."

"Your husband didn't figure into the decision, Mrs. Van Wyck. I am old and tired and maybe a little depressed after a long recovery from cancer. I just ran out of stamina that evening."

She led the way to the entry so he could retrieve her coat. "Spenser wanted to be significant, you know. He was right this time, and no one was listening."

"You may be right in thinking you have the contacts to get behind Linfield's façade."

"Am I that transparent?"

"If you are successful, please call me with what you learn. I am listening."

Childers wrote his new phone number on a card from the table by the door. She plucked the card from his hand.

"If I didn't think you still might be some use to me, I'd slap your face."

He opened the door. "Please accept my condolences, Mrs. Van Wyck."

She drove off in a rental sedan, perched behind the wheel as if it were a Rolls Royce.

Childers went back to his computer to finish his reconciliation. He had spent a lot of time at his computer recently. Linfield's offer was reviewed by e-mail. The approval meeting was held on Skype. A large portion of his net worth had depended on software that could contain who-knew-how-many malicious viruses lurking and ready to strike without warning. An idea began to gnaw at him. He lifted the phone, pressed out a number and fretted through three transfers.

"Levi Weiss."

"Earl Childers, Levi. I just had a visit from Catherine Van Wyck."

"Take the lady with a grain of salt, Earl. She lost her husband. She isn't coping well."

"How should I take the US Marshals Service?" Childers asked. "Protective surveillance is pretty imposing."

"That's been discontinued."

"Why?"

"Three weeks, no action. They can't keep it up forever."

"Did it have anything to do with Hollister?"

"What's eating you, Earl?"

"The purpose of the Hollister buyout is to fund a marketing campaign for the new industrial control system. Today it is on one platform. In two years it may be on dozens. If it is infected with a computer virus now, it may serve as a Trojan horse."

"I hope you're not going to refer me to the *Iliad*."

"The Trojan Horse was never mentioned in Homer's *Iliad*. I believe the usual attribution is Lesches of Mitylene for the building of the horse and Arctinus of Miletus for the sack of Troy. Only fragments of their actual works remain. What we know is mostly from reference and summary."

"Very good, Earl. Very literate."

"Don't you think the government is ignoring an obvious threat?"

"Earl, you beat cancer. You just won the lottery. These are your golden years. Play some golf. Book a cruise. Your only worries should be sand traps and seasickness."

Weiss hung up and left Childers brooding. Health club visits weren't helping his stamina. The doctor he had seen read his medical history and scheduled him for positron emission tomography. The results were still pending. If he were facing another battle with cancer, the next day or two might be all the time he had to come to grips with the events swirling around him. He took time to load the Winchester before he pressed out another number.

The first of Hollister's software engineers had left a voice message that he would be out of town for the remainder of the week. The second number was answered by a woman.

"He's not here," she said with an undercurrent of anger.

"Have you any idea where I could reach him?" Childers asked.

"I wish I did. He was supposed to meet me and my attorney. Your damned company screwed up our marriage, and now it's screwing up our divorce."

"Any idea at all," Childers persisted. "It is important."

"It always is," she snapped. "For you people."

"Possibly for a great number of people," Childers said.

"His stupid phone message said something about having to be out of touch because of the supply boat."

"Was he going to catch the boat out to the platform?"

"I don't know. I don't care anymore. I've been put off and lied to so many times it just doesn't matter anymore."

A call to Hollister established that the supply boat would be leaving that morning for a run to the platform. Childers found a warm coat and put the rifle into the Honda.

The Marshals' sedan in his mirror came as a surprise. Levi Weiss had been wrong. The Winchester was reduced to excess baggage. He retrieved his cell phone to report his new itinerary. The battery was drained. Again. The condition had become chronic since Flores asked him to leave the phone on 24/7. He put it in the car charger. Activating the unfamiliar hands-free function wasn't worth the nuisance. He would be easy enough to follow.

Chapter 23

$\mathcal{V}$ALENTINA FLORES FELT LIKE THE Michelin Man bundled in her bulky storm coat. The wind had risen and gusts sent dead leaves and paper trash scurrying among the cars that crowded the arena parking lot. Moving clouds cast shifting patterns of shadow over the reader board. The event was billed as the Western Regionals. Recommended dress was traditional Argentine or semi-formal. Flores had to dig out her badge to get past security.

The strains of *Blue Tango* filled the facility. There were no empty seats anywhere close to the hardwood where twelve competing couples strutted stylized figures in time to the music. Flores made her way to a table where middle aged women in black mantillas held court.

"I need to locate Alexis Tremaine," she told the one under a sign that said *T through Z.*

The woman checked a cardboard file drawer full of cards. "Couple 118. They are taking the floor next."

Blue Tango faded to a close under a round of applause. The competitors cleared the floor. An MC asked the judges to complete their score sheets. A new group of couples filed on and took positions. The MC called for music and *Jealousy* came from the speakers. Flores was able to identify Tremaine only by the number on her back. The woman looked completely different in the tight fitting dance outfit, marcelled hair and dramatic make-up meant to suggest an Argentine prostitute.

"Let's hear it for your favorites," the MC said.

Of the twelve dance couples crowding the floor, Tremaine and her partner did best in applause. They looked to be first or second in both required steps and floor craft. The music ended with more applause and the dancers cleared off to make room for the next round. Flores pursued Tremaine into a large preparation room packed with costumed dancers.

The smell of sweat and muscle cream brought back memories. A few years ago she might have been half of one of the couples either decompressing from a round of competition or getting ready for one. She no longer competed, but she was still dancing to someone else's music.

Tremaine was perspiring when Flores caught up with her. She excused herself from her partner and took Flores aside.

"I didn't expect to see you here. Is something wrong?"

"I just wanted to be sure you knew that we were shutting down the Childers surveillance," Flores said.

Webster had been adamant that she notify Tremaine in person. She was to report back the exact time and location of the notification, along with any reaction that Tremaine had. All Flores could see was exhaustion and apology.

"Give me a minute to catch my breath."

"That was a demanding routine," Flores said. Even for a younger woman.

"When I started, Tango was a lark and most of the entry fee would go to rent a high-school gymnasium. Now it's all professionally coached and judged. Tomorrow night's finals will be danced in a cabaret setting on cable television."

"I hope you make it."

"Any tips?"

"I haven't been on the floor in six years."

Or done much else for that matter. Flores had allowed her professional life to turn her personal life into a disaster.

Even when it gave her an edge with Bill, she hadn't been able to close. What little time they had together had been limited to fun dates. She hadn't been able to maneuver him into serious talk. She couldn't do anything about that, but she could bail out of the Childers surveillance.

"I just came to be sure you knew we were shutting down and get any reaction you had."

"It shouldn't be a problem. The threat to Childers appears to have come from his position with Hollister. Now that he is no longer a shareholder or Board member, there should be no danger."

Unconditional release. Webster was going to love that.

"Are you leaving today?" Tremaine asked.

The question surprised Flores. A few weeks ago Tremaine had used her to follow the Monterosa woman because she couldn't use an FBI agent. Now she sounded like she couldn't wait to get her out of Dodge. Webster thought Tremaine was 24/7 on top of some critical situation. In fact she was done up in an outlandish costume, strutting and sweating on a hardwood floor, a million miles from any responsibilities. Flores felt like Alice in some bureaucratic Wonderland. At least she was on her way out.

"Tomorrow," she told Tremaine. "My team is down to one Marshal. I have to fill the empty slot in the last shift myself."

Bill hadn't said when he was leaving. He was trying not to act heartbroken that he wouldn't become a permanent part of Linfield's organization. Flores was glad to have him out. She wished Tremaine luck and hustled out to rejoin her partner and relieve the Childers' surveillance team.

The Deputy Marshal's first name was Ed and his last was an Italian nightmare that she had never gotten right. He loved to talk about his three kids. With one officer already dead, the conversations just made her glad nothing had come of the Childers surveillance to put him and the rest of the team in danger.

"Our man is moving," he said as he pulled out of the parking lot. Where is he headed?"

"Didn't he report his itinerary?"

Flores checked her e-mail and voice mail. Nothing from Childers. That wasn't like him. In the weeks since they talked, he had never missed sending a detailed itinerary and never deviated from what he sent. She couldn't forget what happened the last time someone decided he was safe and pulled his protection. She called the surveillance unit for an update on his position and direction.

"Looks like he's headed for the harbor," came the response.

"What's there?" she asked her partner.

"Broken lot freight. Service vessels. Anything small or local. The overseas container traffic goes through Oakland."

Childers had never gone there--at least not while he was under surveillance--and she could think of no reason he would go now. It was just her luck he would decide to break his routine on the last day of the assignment. Flores called the surveillance team and had them designate a rendezvous point.

Ten minutes later Childers' Honda was in sight. The surveillance team had nothing unusual to report and Flores released them to end their shift. Childers parked in a lot next to a pier and got out. Flores unfastened her seatbelt.

"Find a spot as close as you can to his car," she instructed her partner. "I'm going to stay with him."

Outside the sedan nature made its presence felt. Raw wind brought a tang of salt and a few stray drops of rain off the bay. Swirling mist imparted a surreal quality to the movement of men and machines working the dock. Flores pushed her hands into the pockets of her storm coat and set off after Childers.

He seemed to have only a vague idea of where he was going, stopping to ask directions from a longshoreman and then making his way along the bustling pier to a large vessel riding low under a heavy deck load. He went up the gangway and spoke to a man on deck before he disappeared into the superstructure. Flores followed signs to the Harbormaster's office on the second floor of a pier-side building.

The office was all cubicles, with slanted windows that looked down over the harbor. There was no reception desk. She showed her identification to a solidly built white-haired man at a copy machine.

"I need to see the Harbormaster. Or whoever is in charge."

The man had seen a lot of badges in his years and was no longer impressed. "He's away, Missy. Budget meeting. All day, most likely."

She pointed out the window to the boat Childers had boarded. "What is that vessel?"

"That's the *Nourakrina*, Missy."

"Did it just arrive?"

"It's a platform supply vessel, Missy."

"Who is the owner?"

"Maritime leasing company, most likely."

"You must have a record. Who would you call if there was a problem?"

"Title to a vessel is all about taxes and legal liability any more. Nobody sails what they own."

"Who operates it?"

"Company called Hollister."

Childers had sold his interest in Hollister. He was supposed to be out of danger because he was out of the picture.

"Is it scheduled for departure?" Flores asked.

"They just finished loading. Making a run out to Fort Apache."

A chill ran up Flores spine. "What is Fort Apache?"

"Oil drilling platform, Missy. Out on the Continental shelf. Fort Apache. That's what they call it."

Flores bolted out without bothering to thank the man and stopped half way down the stairs. The Maroon Escalade she had seen the night she followed Pilar Monterosa was idling near the gate to the pier. She took the remaining stairs three at a time, sprinted to the surveillance sedan and banged on the driver's window.

Her partner rolled down the glass. "What's up?"

"I'm going to pull Childers off that boat and find out what the hell is going on here." She gave him the color and license number of the Escalade. "If it leaves, you stay with it. I'll call for transport if I need it."

As soon as she questioned Childers, she would drag Tremaine's ass off the dance floor and read her in on the situation. It was a long sprint down the dock, dodging forklifts and cargo trams. Flores reached the gangway of the boat out of breath and climbed to the top.

A young seaman blocked her way. He looked a bit nervous, but his tone was emphatic.

"Sorry, Ma'am. No one allowed on board."

Flores' badge was buried inside her coat. Maybe she could just talk her way past the young sailor.

"A man came aboard," she began, and discovered she didn't have enough voice to carry over the cacophony from the dock. She took a minute to catch her breath.

The crewman glanced nervously along his shoulder. A door was open in a nearby metal bulkhead. A Kalashnikov assault rifle pointed at her from the shadows of a gangway inside the superstructure.

Flores' heart sank. She had just committed the ultimate law enforcement blunder. Instead of setting up surveillance, properly briefing her partner and calling for back-up, she had forgotten she was a member of a team and charged headlong into a situation.

"Come," a male voice ordered from the darkness of the gangway. "You. Woman. Come here. Come now."

There was little she could do. Her service automatic was securely zipped and buttoned under her heavy coat. The noise and bustle of the dock would cover any sound she made. Even a gunshot might pass unnoticed in the clatter. Legs stiff with fear carried her to the doorway and she stepped into the dimness of the gangway.

A hand yanked the bag off her shoulder. The contents were emptied onto the metal floor. A heel made short work of her cell phone. Men crowded around her. They smelled foreign but her eyes will still adjusting and she couldn't see them clearly.

There was a brief conversation in what sounded to her like Arabic. It dawned on her that it was forbidden by Islam for a male to physically search a female. If these were hard-core nut cases, there was a chance they might not find her automatic or her credentials. Whatever happened, she had to keep her head in the game.

"Who are you?" a man demanded.

"Cook," she blurted on impulse.

"Cook? What do you mean cook?"

"Food preparation. On the drilling platform. The cook is sick. I got a last minute call. I have to go out and fill in."

"You lie."

The man was military in carriage. He thrust his face close and she could make out a scar like a tear at the corner of one eye. She realized she had made two more mistakes. If she was a replacement on the platform, she should have luggage. Claiming a call was even worse. If they picked up her cell phone for a close look, they would see it was marked *Property of US Marshals Service*. Her only hope was that a poker face might cover a thin bluff.

More foreign gibberish.

"Go with him," the man who spoke English ordered.

She was prodded along the gangway with the muzzle of a Kalashnikov. If this scow had a kitchen or a galley or whatever it was called, they might put her to work. She would have to move fast. It wouldn't take them long to notice that she had the culinary skills of a traffic cone.

She had no idea what had become of Childers, and finding him was no longer a priority. She needed to get ashore and notify the Coast Guard. Even if it meant swimming. Once the boat left the harbor with a gang of pirates in control, there wouldn't be much hope of getting off alive.

Chapter 24

HILIP LINFIELD'S SAN FRANCISCO HEADQUARTERS resembled a symphony hall after the final concert of the season. The movers had everything upside down, carting away the rental furniture. The project staff was cramming weeks' worth of work into bankers' boxes. Linfield was organizing the agreements he would deliver to The Prince's functionaries when his cell phone rang.

"Elmer, what do you have for me?"

"Are you alone?"

Linfield was in no mood for histrionics. He had been too long discharging his primary responsibilities by video-conference and email. Now that the Hollister buyout had been consummated, he needed to clear up the final details and return his full attention to managing his firm.

"Elmer, I simply asked you to find out what interest the Government had in my activities. Now, I don't think that calls for any cloak and dagger nonsense."

"Did you know a man named Spenser Van Wyck?"

"Who?"

"Bank officer. Specialized in international finance."

Two movers jockeyed a transport dolly into the office and began maneuvering it toward Linfield's desk. He tried to shoo them out, but they were lost and unreachable in a world of ear bud rap. He put the documents into a briefcase and carried that and the phone to the window.

A darkening sky told him more of northern California's god-awful weather was blowing in off the Pacific. Another reason he wanted to put this phase of the project behind him and get home.

"What about him?" Linfield asked.

"He was killed in that condominium firebombing in San Francisco."

Linfield could summon only vague memories of news coverage. "I didn't know the fellow."

"How about his wife?"

"What are you suggesting?"

"Apparently she has been on her cell phone most of the afternoon. Morning your time, I guess."

"Elmer, I am happy to grant you that women and cell phones are an unfortunate combination, but what does that have to do with me?"

"She's been asking a lot of questions, Philip. She believes her husband's death was connected with this Hollister buyout."

Linfield threw a nervous glance at the movers. They were absorbed in wrestling his desk onto the transport dolly. He lowered his voice.

"The Hollister acquisition is a done deal. It has already cleared escrow."

"I don't think this broad is interested in the finer points of business, Philip."

"Why hasn't she spoken up earlier?"

"Apparently she has been poking around for weeks, trying to learn why her husband was killed. Her last stop was San Francisco, to see this Earl Childers character."

Linfield felt his hand squeeze the phone and knew he had to control his anger. "I need specifics on Childers' involvement."

"He was supposed to be attending a meeting with Van Wyck when the bombing occurred. That's what initially put him under Marshals Service protection."

"How is that connected with Hollister?"

"I haven't been able to get a fix on the Government's thinking. A couple of sources told me not to ask. With that in mind, I thought you ought to know the Van Wyck woman has been raising holy hell in official circles."

"What do you mean, raising holy hell?"

"She comes from an old family, Philip. This broad is connected."

"Don't lecture me on that, Elmer. I've been living with it for the last twenty odd years."

"Not at this level, Philip. Catherine Van Wyck has played a lot of footsie in her time. She can threaten some very important marriages. That alone is going to give her ideas traction."

"What ideas are you talking about?"

"Did you cut a deal with some Arab Prince to fund the Hollister deal?"

"Elmer, we can't go seeing terrorists under the bed in every business arrangement with the Middle East. For God's sake, this fellow is a London educated professional, not some blathering Imam from a desert mosque."

"Don't bark at me, Philip. I'm just trying to tell you what this woman is spreading."

"Are you suggesting the Government will come down with 9/11 fever and believe anything she says?"

"Apparently the theory is based on material her husband sourced from followers of sects inimical to your Prince, so it may be a bit over the top, but coming from multiple sources suggests it might not be entirely rumor."

"I presume you are going to let me in on this mysterious theory?"

"The Prince bought Hollister to get control of their new industrial control software. He intends to infect it with a virus, market it widely and when it is in place on enough oil platforms, trigger the virus to cause a massive environmental catastrophe and energy shortage, bringing the west to its knees. Long story short, he is declaring cyber war, and you are leading his shock troops."

"Ridiculous," Linfield said.

The movers jockeyed the desk out of his office and he closed the door behind them.

"Cyber war is waged by major governments. Even the combined resources of the US and Israel were only partly successful in slowing the Iranian nuclear weapons program."

"Are you absolutely certain?"

"Elmer, we're not talking about China or Russia. No Arab organization or government has the breadth and depth of intellectual sophistication required. For all their wealth and education, they are still Bedouins, no more than three or four generations off the backs of camels."

"Maybe so," Elmer said, "but Catherine Van Wyck is pushing the idea hard. This is one bad bitch, Philip, and you will have to deal with the situation."

This afternoon's document delivery was the precursor to release of the next increment of funding. The start of Hollister's marketing campaign. Even a rumor that the software had been compromised could be catastrophic.

"Thank you for the heads-up," Linfield said. "I would appreciate the names of anyone she has spoken with. She is not the only one capable of exerting influence."

Linfield ended the call still unsure why he was under Federal scrutiny. Cyber terror was a logical threat for a man in Childers' position to raise if he were on some sort of vendetta. The timing would allow him to both collect his payout and take a swipe at Linfield for whatever grievance he might be harboring. But the government wouldn't ramp up a counter-terror investigation on the unsupported word of a single informant. There had to be more to it. Linfield summoned the young Montgomery fellow.

"Sorry for the inconvenience," he said, "but I need to deliver final documents. I hope you won't mind collecting the keys to the rental car and driving."

"Right away, Sir."

The Prince's delegate had been apologetic, but explained that he would be detained by an inspection of property in the area and asked if Linfield could come to his lodging for this afternoon's meeting. What had seemed a nuisance now presented an opportunity to ask a few discreet questions.

Highway 1 south of the city was described by the tourist brochure as scenic. Desolate would have been more accurate. The asphalt narrowed to two lanes, squeezed between rugged hills on one side and a rocky shore on the other. The ocean ran white-capped and turbulent under a dark sky. Montgomery had to hold the rental sedan against buffeting gusts of wind. Linfield distrusted GPS and unfolded a map on his lap.

"I expect you'll be glad to get home," he said. "As I recall, you brought a rather attractive young woman to our get-acquainted function."

"Tina," Montgomery said with no discernible emotion.

Law enforcement was a blue collar career, and any dalliance with the Flores woman would be no more than passing amusement for someone of his family standing and prospects. The question was whether she was participating for personal or professional reasons.

"I hope you've been able to stay in touch."

"Actually, she's been on assignment in San Francisco."

"That's convenient." Linfield hoped his feigned surprise wasn't too obvious.

"I haven't seen much of her. We've both been pretty busy."

"You know, I don't recall hearing exactly what sort of work she did."

"She's a Deputy US Marshal."

"Indeed," Linfield said. "And what is she doing in San Francisco?"

"Some sort of witness protection, I think. She isn't allowed to talk much about her work, although I got the impression she was frustrated with this assignment."

She sounded like a low level tactical operative who had been told no more than she needed to know. Beyond that was the question of how much she had told Montgomery.

"Who was the witness?" Linfield asked.

"She didn't say directly, although she did once ask if I knew anything about Earl Childers."

"The same gentleman who was on Hollister's board before the buyout?"

"I believe so."

"Any idea what the specific threat against him is?"

"I believe he testified in a criminal trial in New York. It might have something to do with that."

Articles surrounding the New York criminal case had first alerted Linfield to the investment potential in Hollister. If the threat came from the trial, then it pre-dated Linfield's interest in Hollister. Childers might have been privy to something amiss within the company. Linfield might have become enmeshed only because he moved to acquire Hollister.

That would exculpate The Prince. He was just one of several investors to respond to Linfield's proposal to acquire and expand Hollister. The only one who hadn't flinched at the cost and risk involved. Elmer's view of The Prince's intentions was a sour note of hyperbole, but there might be some misguided souls in government who could be goaded into taking action that would compromise Hollister's prospects.

The Prince had to be advised of the situation. It was only a matter of time before he began picking up hints from his own information sources.

Just broaching the subject with no more information than Linfield had would be risky. Particularly dealing through intermediaries who would certainly filter any message he might pass to avoid offending their patron. Linfield needed to learn as much as possible before his next meeting with The Prince.

A peal of thunder came from the distance and raindrops began to splash on the windshield. Montgomery turned on the wipers. Linfield consulted the map.

"I think we'll want the next turn off."

A blacktop road took them to the crest of a bluff commanded by two stories of Spanish style motor hotel. An ornate façade and a preponderance of high-end vehicles in the parking lot suggested an out of the way retreat for the well to do. Montgomery pulled up under a porte-cochere. A valet in a matador's costume took charge of the sedan. Montgomery carried the briefcase of documents and stayed a respectful half step behind Linfield.

The lobby décor had an overpowering Iberian flavor, probably meant to offer vicarious escape to a past when over-privileged Spanish grandees exercised baronial dominion over old California. Linfield announced them at the reception desk and gave the name of the man he was to see.

"Will you wait, please, Sir?"

The clerk's telephone call brought a surprise. The motherly Chinese woman Linfield met on his New York visit with The Prince bustled into the lobby shedding raindrops from an umbrella.

"Mrs. Yuan," Linfield recalled.

"So very nice to see you again, Mr. Linfield."

She extended a hand and he shook it briefly.

"Does your presence mean that I will have the honor of meeting with The Prince?"

"His Highness is so looking forward to seeing you. There is so much to discuss, and so little time."

Chapter 25

EARL CHILDERS WAS GROGGY AND only vaguely aware that he had been deposited in a windowless compartment within the superstructure of the *Nourakrina*. He touched the side of his head. Pain made him wince and brought memories of a blow from a rifle butt.

He recalled boarding the vessel and finding his way to the bridge. There he encountered several armed men. They were as surprised by his arrival as he was by their presence. Young and full of adrenaline, they reacted instantly. His ribs ached where he had been shoved against the control console.

Only one seemed to speak English. He demanded to know who Childers was and why he had come aboard. Childers explained that he was looking for one of Hollister's software engineers. The man demanded Childers' cell phone. When Childers remembered he had left it in the car charger, the man called him a liar. He was punched, kicked and searched.

The next minutes were a fuzzy recollection of being half dragged and half stumbling along a gangway. He was hauled through a door, shoved into a chair and left to gather a sense of his surroundings.

Spartan furniture, a coffee maker, a rack of magazines and a cheap CD player suggested this was a crew lounge. The only other chair was occupied by a man in a pea coat and an officer's cap. Years at sea had hardened and lined his face and left his expression stoic. His chair was directly across the compartment from Childers', separated by the width of an empty couch. He watched Childers without moving a muscle.

The English speaking captor strode in. He was a thickly built man with military bearing obvious under a new London Fog raincoat. A scar drooped from the corner of one eye like a menacing tear, an expression of sorrow for anyone who crossed him.

"No talking," he ordered, looking first at Childers then at the officer. "If you talk, he shoots."

He strode out, shutting the door behind him. The man who remained to enforce silence between Childers and the ship's officer was not much older than the draftees Childers had led in Vietnam; perhaps a foot soldier in one of the newer and even murkier conflicts that had arisen since.

The youth's features were Semitic. His raincoat hung open over a rumpled business suit to allow access to folding stock Kalashnikov assault rifle supported on a sling. Around his neck hung a visitors' pass allowing him access to Fort Apache. An earpiece kept him in touch with activity outside the compartment.

Time crept past, each second ticked off by the throbbing in Childers's head. He could taste blood inside his mouth. He regretted not calling his itinerary in to Flores. He didn't recall seeing his surveillance when he arrived at the harbor. He could only hope they hadn't ended his protection and dropped off.

The guard heard something on his earpiece and opened the door. Valentina Flores was pushed in and Childers' last hope of help evaporated. She seemed to be making a point of not recognizing him. He took his cue from her.

The English speaking captor stepped in behind her.

"Sit," he told Flores.

She sat on the couch.

"No talking," the man said. "If you talk, he will shoot."

The man closed the compartment door and left the three of them under the scrutiny of the guard. A minute of nervous silence passed, and another and another. Then the vibration of the ship's diesels broke the stillness. Movement became perceptible. They were pulling away from the dock. The guard came alert and then went out without a word.

Flores was on her feet immediately. She tried the door handle. It didn't move. She turned on the officer.

"Do you have a key?"

He eyed her with an expression that bordered on amusement. "And who might you be?"

"My name is Valentina Flores. I am a Deputy United States Marshal."

"And my maiden aunt belongs to the PTA."

She dug her identification out from under her coat. "And you are?"

"Corrigan. First officer."

"And the men with the guns?"

"We weren't properly introduced."

"What do they want?"

"Well, now, they didn't say exactly, but from the questions they were asking and the instructions they were giving, I expect part of the plan is to take over the drilling platform."

Flores turned on Childers. "What do you know about that?"

"Nothing."

"You must have had some reason to board the vessel."

Childers summarized his conversation with Catherine Van Wyck, and his concern that the new Hollister control system might become a Trojan horse for a computer virus.

"That doesn't make sense," Flores said. "If they wanted to infect the software, they would insert the malicious code through a robotic network. They wouldn't physically attack the platform. That would draw attention and defeat the purpose of a secretly embedded virus."

Childers recalled that Nisham had said the hardware was immune to robotic attack, but otherwise Flores was right. Even if access to the hardware was required, insertion through bribery, subterfuge or infiltration would minimize the risk of discovery.

"Do all these people have platform visitor's passes?" he asked Corrigan.

"And who might you be, old timer?"

"My name is Earl Childers. I am, or was, a member of Hollister's Board of Directors."

There was no mirth in Corrigan's laugh. "The Management and the Government. Aren't people like you supposed to sit behind desks until the trouble is over and then conduct a thorough inquiry to find some poor soul to blame?"

This was no time to be baited into a silly labor-management squabble. "How many are there?" Childers asked.

"Twelve. Claimed they'd come for some kind of tour on the platform."

"Then why risk hijacking the vessel? Why not wait until they were on the platform to make their move?"

"Captain Peterson wouldn't take them out."

"Why not?"

"Too dangerous. There's a weather front moving in. It'll be tricky enough getting the supplies transferred. Peterson ordered them off the ship. Next thing we knew, they had automatic weapons pointed at us."

That wasn't good news. Their captors' plan was going wrong from the start. Childers recalled that there were two Marshals assigned to watch over him.

"Marshal Flores," he asked, "what became of your partner?"

"We had to split up. It could be hours before he misses me."

Corrigan seemed oddly satisfied. "We'll be at the platform before then."

Flores turned on him. "What sort of weapons do you have on board?"

"No weapons on a merchant vessel, lady. Not allowed. Violation of the International Safe Harbor Act. If you're the law, you ought to know that."

Flores compressed her lips. "Any chance these people will get seasick during the trip? I mean, how bad will the weather get."

"There's a couple of oriental characters that might get a little green around the gills," Corrigan said. "The rest have sea legs. Might be merchant seamen. Foreign navy experience maybe. Blue water sailors for sure. You can always tell."

"What about radio codes?" She asked. "Will the Captain be able to signal we've been hijacked without the pirates knowing?"

"This gang is way ahead of you, lady. From the orders I heard them give Captain Peterson they know the frequencies, the codes, the harbor departure procedures. Everything."

A sense of the situation began to penetrate the throbbing in Childers' head. The men who had taken the boat were well equipped and organized. The project had been meticulously planned and prepared. Two of the participants were oriental. That might or might not have something to do with the Chinaman who was mentioned during the attempt on Childers' life. The thoroughness involved might also mean collusion from inside Hollister. None of which addressed the immediate danger.

"Our best bet," Childers decided, "is when we dock at the platform."

"Best bet for what?" Corrigan demanded.

"To get the boat away from these people."

"That's crazy."

"I've been on the platform during the docking routine," Childers said. "They'll need all hands on deck to perform the maneuver. The minute it's done, they'll need most of their force to swarm onto the platform to take control. That will leave one or two guards on the boat, with the whole crew on deck. If we can shove the guards overboard and undock, there will be nothing the men on the platform can do."

Corrigan looked from Childers to Flores and back. There was a sardonic twist to his mouth.

"Funny how old men and women always want to pick a fight, but it's the young men that get stuck taking the chances."

"Do you have a better idea?" Childers asked.

"Wait it out," Corrigan said. "Leave the rough stuff to the professionals."

"A little late for that, isn't it?"

"Nobody attacks a drilling platform just for the fun of it. They have to contact someone to make their demands."

"What then?" Childers asked.

"The military know oil platforms are targets," Corrigan said. "They rehearse what to do if one is taken. Navy Seals held a practice raid on Fort Apache not two months ago."

"That won't help us," Childers said. "Once these people get access to the platform, they have no use for us."

"How do they get off without us?" Corrigan asked.

"How do you know they're planning to? All the 9/11 gang wanted to do was take as many with them as they could."

Corrigan had no answer.

"And if they do want to get off," Childers said, "they'll have other transportation lined up. They wouldn't make a run for it in a heavily loaded supply boat."

"My crew are merchant seamen, not soldiers."

"All right, so it's not in their union contract. What are they going to do? Go on strike? Wave picket signs?"

"Now look here, Mister, I'm First Officer on this ship. The authority is mine, not yours."

"So exercise it. Take the guns away from these goons."

Anger flared in Corrigan's eyes. Flores stepped between the two men.

"Stop it," she said, and faced Corrigan. "How many in the crew?"

"Captain. First officer. Chief Engineer. Fourteen all other rates. Enginemen. Deck hands. Loaders. Family men who didn't ask for any of this."

"We're not going to endanger--."

The door burst open. Five crewmen were herded in at gunpoint.

"No talking," the English speaking captor said. "All sit."

Flores sat on the couch. Crewmen were seated on the floor wherever there was an empty space of wall.

"Stay still," the captor ordered. "No talking."

He left two guards, both with automatic weapons. The boat began to roll. They were at sea; out of the harbor, on the way to the platform. Any excess crew would be held at gunpoint until they were needed for docking.

The situation was clear, but that was as far as Childers' thinking could take him. His head was pounding and fatigue weighed down his mind until he was aware only that his eyelids were growing heavy.

Chapter 26

ALENTINA FLORES HAD NEVER SEEN an actual offshore drilling platform but she remembered the endless television coverage of the *Deep Water Horizon* disaster. The platform burned for weeks, dumped millions of gallons of oil into the Gulf of Mexico and deposited tarry ooze along hundreds of miles of pristine shoreline. That was unintentional. Whatever was going to happen on Fort Apache would be calculated to produce maximum and perhaps irreversible damage. Flores was the only law enforcement officer on scene. That made her responsible to stop it.

Her chances looked slim. The service automatic concealed under her coat would be no match for the terrorists' assault weapons, and it was only a matter of time until they learned she was a Deputy US Marshal. Eventually her partner would report to the Marshals' office. When she didn't answer her cell phone, they would trace her to the vessel and try to contact her by radio. The terrorists controlled the bridge.

There was no help available on board. Corrigan was tough, experienced, disciplined, but his attitude toward management suggested he was a product of the decks rather than the Merchant Marine Academy. A set of first officer's papers testified to initiative and intelligence, but his loyalty was to his shipmates. He would take no risk unless they were in danger.

Captain Peterson was a question mark. Judging from the reaction of the crew, he had issued orders not to resist. Flores had no way to know whether he had a plan, or was just playing for time.

The crew she could only judge from the men seated on the floor. The oldest of the five was in his fifties, and years of labor under orders appeared to have left him resigned to whatever fate held in store for him. Three were in their thirties. One looked Korean, short and taciturn, and two South Asian, perhaps Malay or Pakistani. Men lucky enough to have green cards and probably unwilling to put their good fortune at risk. Merchant sailors with families, working to make ends meet. None looked to have any stomach for rebellion. All seemed ready to wait this out and get back to their workaday cares.

The youngest was the sailor who had tried to warn her against boarding. He was in his twenties, stocky, roughly dressed, unkempt blond hair curling out from under a black woolen cap. He looked like someone who wanted to save up for his dream car but wasn't going to let that get in the way of a good time on Saturday night. The enforced silence left him chafing. He raided his pockets, came up empty and nudged the stolid Korean who sat beside him.

"Hey, Bro, you got a smoke?"

The two guards stiffened. They were even younger than the seaman. Five years ago they would have been kids kicking a soccer ball around. Now they were zealots with heads full of indoctrination, arteries full of adrenaline and fingers dancing on loaded Kalashnikovs.

One leveled his weapon.

"No talk!"

The young seaman grinned. "Lighten up, Bro. I just want a——"

The guard's rifle discharged a two round burst. In the confines of the crew lounge the rapid-fire concussions were ear-splitting. The two rounds slammed into the young seaman's chest inches apart, ripping through and hitting the bulkhead behind him with solid thunks. He jerked spasmodically and slumped back against the bulkhead. His mouth moved feebly, but no sound came out.

Flores remembered the concept of s sucking chest wound from training. The lungs collapsed under the pressure of inrushing air and the victim could neither speak nor breathe. Death would follow quickly without immediate action. The entry and exit wounds had to be blocked with impervious material. Pressure had to be applied to ensure an airtight seal.

The two guards appeared to know none of that. They had been told to shoot anyone who spoke but apparently had been given no instructions what to do after the shooting was over. In their minds they stood as two martyrs against many infidels. They glanced around in fear and confusion, ready to engage anyone who reacted.

No one moved or spoke.

The young seaman grew still with a look of disbelief on his face. The last vestige of life drained from his eyes. The other crewmen were stunned by the suddenness with which violence had erupted and the finality of its aftermath.

Corrigan's expression said he knew that he had lost more than a man. He had lost the aura of command that underlay his status as a ship's officer.

Flores sat with her ears ringing and the stench of burned nitro powder filling her nostrils and knew she had lost the sense of order and authority that went with being a Deputy US Marshal. A man had been shot dead in front of her and she had been able to do nothing. Impotence fueled anger.

Tremaine's words echoed in Flores' mind. Keep a lid on the adrenaline. Think controlled situation. She couldn't change the past. Any sudden action might provoke more violence. She had to get a grip on her emotions to be ready for whatever came next.

The door burst open. The terrorist leader came in. He snarled something in Arabic. The man who had fired blurted a jittery response. The leader glared at Corrigan and the remaining crew.

"You just shot him," Corrigan said. "For no reason."

"You were told to remain silent," the terrorist snapped.

"He just wanted a smoke. That's all. Just a smoke."

There was general muttering of support from the crew. This was a bad time for a show of bravado.

"Silence!"

The two guards leveled their rifles to enforce the order. The terrorist chief stepped to Corrigan's chair and loomed over him.

"You are officer. You must control your men. My man just followed orders. It is your fault your man is dead."

How the dumb shit expected Corrigan to control anything with a gun in his face was beyond Flores' comprehension. His outburst suggested that circumstances were getting away from him. The terrorists had planned to bluff their way aboard the platform with visitors' badges. Seizing the vessel was a last minute act of desperation.

Childers was probably right about one thing. The terrorists needed maximum deck crew presence to dock with the platform. Any crewman they lost raised the risk of failure. Murdering the crew to put down a rebellion would doom their raid as surely as the rebellion itself.

The terrorist chief must know that he was running a dangerously thin bluff. If it went south on him, he was liable to panic and plunge the whole operation into some lunatic martyrdom. He pointed at the two men flanking the dead seaman, the Korean and a South Asian.

"Bring him!"

The two men looked to Corrigan for orders. Some combination of habit, loyalty and economic survival had dulled their fear and left the chain of authority intact. Corrigan was smart enough to see the futility of resisting now and nodded. They stood and caught their comrade under his armpits. Lifting his considerable dead weight required exertion, even for two strong men. Moving him was clumsy. They half-carried, half-dragged him out after the terrorist.

The two guards remained at the door, their Kalashnikovs leveled. Their eyes were tense and shifting, ready to meet any threat.

The two crewmen returned glum-faced in a few minutes to be locked in with the rest, and with the guards. They sagged obediently into sitting positions against the wall. It took only a head motion to signal that the dead man had been thrown overboard.

Silence ruled.

The coppery smell of blood mingled with residual powder smoke to leave little doubt about the potential outcome of the hijacking. The seamen looked restive, as if they wanted to jump the two terrorists and risk the consequences. Automatic weapons in a metal box could produce carnage even if they succeeded. Corrigan's expression said wait.

Flores feared what he might be thinking. If he didn't assert control, he would lose his only opportunity. That required action. Childers' proposal to jump the terrorists remaining on the boat just after the main party had swarmed the platform was the only idea on the table.

It would produce a confused situation that could get more men killed on the boat and the platform. The irony was that it might buy Flores her only opportunity to do what she knew had to be done.

Flores' priority had to be the threat to the platform. The only hope of raising help was the radio on the bridge. If she could seize control, however briefly, the platform could be warned and a distress signal sent. Good luck with that. The guards would shoot her if she twitched or let out a peep. She would have no opening until the situation changed, and there was no immediate change in sight.

Corrigan sat stoic and unmoving, his crewmen cowed. No help there. Childers' had made his contribution. He had pointed out the terrorists' Achilles heel. Now he sat slumped and drained.

Flores and Childers were excess to the docking process and no more than a nuisance to the terrorists. Throwing the two of them overboard was the simple solution, but that might spook the crew even further. If it was in the cards, it would already have happened. The real danger came when the terrorists learned who she was. Once she was upgraded from nuisance to threat, all bets were off. Every passing minute increased the risk, and every minute she spent thinking about it raised the risk that her nerves would show and betray her before the inevitable radio call. She needed to think about something else. Keep her head in the game. Analyze the situation. Develop a plan.

Best case, the terrorists would just lock Childers and her in the crew lounge alone when they reached the platform, as they had done before. A surreptitious glance at the lock gave her some hope. It was anything but robust. Probably just something to keep the crew from idling when they should be on duty. A couple of well placed rounds from her Glock should blow out the cylinder and free her to make a try for the bridge.

Worst case, she would be taken on deck during the docking and kept under the eyes and the guns of the terrorists. All she could do was hope for the best and wait for whatever opening the situation gave her. How long before the vessel made its way to the platform and how suddenly events might unfold she couldn't predict. The relentless pitching and rolling wasn't doing her stomach any favors, but she had to hold herself together.

Chapter 27

HILIP LINFIELD FELT THE AIR in the lobby shake with the roll of thunder. The Chinese woman's confirmation that he would be meeting The Prince was even less welcome then the onslaught of wind-driven rain that machine-gunned the lobby windows. There would be no time to devise a strategy. The encounter would be all sight reading and improvisation.

Mrs. Yuan tapped on the registration desk. "Carlos, we must have umbrellas for our guests."

Linfield drew Montgomery a few steps away and spoke quietly. "Best if you stay in the background. Low profile. Speak only if spoken to. This is not the most balanced fellow, and he may come up with some rather outrageous puffery. We can discuss any concerns you have after the meeting."

"Yes, Sir."

There was an undertone of eagerness in Montgomery's voice. The fellow realized he was about to get his first real glimpse into the upper echelons of finance.

Mrs. Yuan led them out into the storm. Linfield held his umbrella against the wind and angled it for what little protection it offered from the slanting rain. An asphalt path took them to an area of bungalows secluded from the main complex by strategically planted hedges. Linfield's shoes squished through puddles and his trouser legs grew sodden beneath the hem of his raincoat.

Their destination was the most remote of the bungalows. The two thugs Linfield remembered from Manhattan were waiting to pat them down. Montgomery had no experience raising funds on the international market, and the precautions that sometimes went with it. Linfield shed his raincoat and managed a reassuring smile.

The Prince waited in a spacious living room, seated in a throne-like gondola chair, decked out in full Arab regalia. Behind him was a panoramic array of windows. Rain came on gusts of wind, alternately running down the glass in waves, like gelatin, and then clearing for a glimpse out over the white capped ocean. The darkness and fury of the storm gave emphasis to the sinister cast of The Prince's lopsided features.

"Good afternoon, Mr. Linfield. I apologize for the subterfuge, but security requirements dictate that my itinerary remain confidential."

"A pleasure as always, Your Highness," Linfield said. "I presume this establishment was selected because you own it?"

"My firms are broadly invested in the hospitality industry. It eases the burden of travel. I have always had a fondness for Iberian motif. Moorish culture is still evident in Spain, a footprint on the sands of time for now, perhaps an omen of the future."

No point reminding the fellow that Charles Martel had crushed the Saracen armies at the Battle of Tours in AD 832 and relegated the first Muslim dream of world domination to the rubbish heap. Or that it was the King of Spain who installed the Templars on Malta to blunt the later Ottoman expansion. Linfield's best approach was to let the fellow rant until it became clear why he had come in person on a trivial errand better left to subordinates.

"Mrs. Yuan," The Prince said, "Mr. Linfield and I will be served now. I believe we will also require an additional box lunch."

Linfield felt a chair pushed against the backs of his legs. Wet trouser legs clung as he sat down. Being relegated to the status of an additional box lunch might rankle Montgomery, but hopefully he would be smart enough to accept the role of spectator for its instructional value. Linfield had eaten his own share of rubber chicken learning the business.

Two Latin men in catering uniforms carried in a table and set it between Linfield and the Prince. A linen table cloth was laid with flourish. It was intended as theatre, but came off as irony; staunch

Catholics setting out table service before a Muslim Prince. Perhaps that was the sort of thing that fed whatever fantasies the fellow harbored.

"I see no reason to sacrifice civilized living to the demands of business," The Prince said. "You have the documents?"

He extended his arm without looking around. Montgomery put the briefcase in his outstretched hand.

"I believe," he said, squaring the paperwork neatly on the table, "that Your Highness will find everything satisfactory."

Mrs. Yuan collected them and took the documents around to set before The Prince. He ignored them to sample a piece of fruit from the platter set before him.

"Of course, they leave me in nominal and you in effective control of the enterprise," he said, and smiled. "Your reputation precedes you, Mr. Linfield. You have done this trick before."

"Hardly control, Your Highness," Linfield said. "Merely enough operational flexibility to ensure efficient prosecution of the objectives of the venture."

"Don't bother equivocating," the Prince said. "Your role in this enterprise was never intended to be more than window dressing."

"Excuse me?" Linfield said.

"To avoid suspicion, the Hollister acquisition required an American of integrity and political influence. A middle-eastern presence might have attracted attention from your government."

Linfield grew uneasy. It was just possible the chatter Elmer had picked up might to have some foundation in fact. Probing was in order.

"I learned just this morning," Linfield said, "that the Hollister acquisition is indeed under government scrutiny."

"Scrutiny of what sort," The Prince inquired.

"There is apparently a rumor," Linfield said, "and as far as I know it is only a rumor, that Hollister's industrial control software may be used as a platform for cyber-infiltration."

A satisfied smile crept across The Prince's face. He balanced a slice of cheese on a small square of bread and chewed contentedly.

"Anyone who believes this to be a simple-minded cyber-infiltration," he said, "has not the slightest grasp of the scope or scale of what is contemplated."

"The concept of a Trojan Horse is well understood," Linfield said.

"Old school," The Prince said. "Is that an American term?"

"Yes."

"Mr. Linfield, the days of pilfered passwords and migratory viruses is past. We have had Hollister's source code for months. We are current on all updates. The kernel of our code has been written in tight integration. It is indistinguishable from Hollister's operating code. Once it is installed, Hollister's system does not simply host the virus. It becomes the virus."

Elmer was right.

The fellow had not only hatched some lunatic scheme, he was boasting about it. Linfield needed to head him off before he sabotaged the project. Best to project an air of calm until he could determine exactly what the fellow had in mind.

"Installation," Linfield said, helping himself to some cheese and bread, "will be problematic with the Government alert to your plan."

"Quite the contrary, it will be done under the nose of the Government. If fact, it requires their assistance, although they will provide it quite unwittingly."

Linfield said nothing. He wondered if the fellow might be beyond reasoning with.

"Do I confuse you, Mr. Linfield? Perhaps that is understandable. You are not in possession of a key fact. You see, installation and testing of code requires physical access to the administrative hardware. We must gain control of the one offshore platform where the software is currently operating and do the work there."

"Impossible," Linfield said. "Platform access is restricted."

"Unfortunately," The Prince said, "we will need to resort to violence to overcome that restriction."

"You would be found out."

"Indeed we shall. In fact, the plan depends on it. You see, your Government expects that hostile forces will one day assault an offshore platform. They rehearse for such an eventuality on a regular basis. So we shall give them what they anticipate. We will assault the platform, seizing control for the time we need, and then when the US military counter-attacks, we will withdraw by preplanned routing and grant them a victory they can trumpet on the television news, leaving behind the modified system."

"They're not fools," Linfield said. "They will check everything on the platform, code included, for tampering."

"A thorough check of the code will require line by line comparison with the master copy held by Hollister. By the time they make their request, the master will have been substituted with a matching copy of what was installed and tested on the platform."

"The developers will know," Linfield said. "They wrote the code."

"Thanks to you," The Prince said, "the developers, who were also shareholders in the firm, have sold their interest to me. They will simply be replaced."

"You do seem to have put some thought into all this," Linfield conceded.

"The overall concept has been in development since US/Israeli efforts against the Iranian nuclear program established a general level of feasibility. I was casting about for some means of implementation when you came along with the Hollister proposal. It was an ideal fit. Perhaps it is a touch of hubris on my part, but I like to think of your fortuitous arrival as Allah's blessing on the enterprise."

Logic would get Linfield nowhere with this fellow. It was time for a firm hand.

"I'm afraid I can't allow it," he said.

"Mr. Linfield, I have not taken the trouble to explain all this to you simply for amusement. You have a role to play, and you will play it."

"I will not be used in anything that harms the United States."

"We have no wish to harm the United States, Mr. Linfield. Merely to bring it into conformance with the just and righteous principles of Islam."

"No."

"A bit late for refusal," The Prince said with a gesture at the windows and the storm tossed Pacific Ocean. "The wheels are already in motion."

Before Linfield could ask what the fellow meant, the Chinese woman bustled in. She went directly to The Prince's chair, put her back to Linfield and spoke in The Prince's ear. The Prince waved her aside.

"Something has come up and I must excuse myself to take a call," he informed Linfield. "Please go ahead with your meal."

The fellow stood and swept out of the room with the Chinese woman in his wake. Linfield motioned and Montgomery came to his chair and went down on one knee with a nervous glance at the two thugs guarding the door.

"Limited English, if any," Linfield said in a low voice. "This discussion could get ugly. Much of what you hear may be disturbing. It is important that you do not react, or show emotion."

"What does this character want?" Montgomery asked.

His voice had the indignation often born of a prep school sense of entitlement. Linfield couldn't afford to have him take some foolish stand in the mistaken belief he was doing the right thing.

"The trick will be to get the fellow to turn all his cards face up before we show any of ours," Linfield said.

"We do have cards, then?"

"I set this Hollister business in motion, and it will be up to me to control it."

"And them?" Montgomery glanced again at the thugs.

"To be dealt with as necessary. Best to return to your chair. We don't want to raise any red flags."

Montgomery withdrew.

The Prince returned and seated himself. His expression was no longer serene. Stress in the small muscles of his face suggested something had happened to upset his plans.

"Things are moving a bit prematurely," he said. "We must accelerate our discussion of the details of your participation in coming events."

Chapter 28

Earl Childers shook his head to clear the fog of sleep. Over the past weeks he had developed a routine of afternoon chair naps to deal with the fatigue that continued to dog him. He was dismayed that exhaustion and habit had overcome his sense of danger and he had dozed off. Something must have awakened him.

The other prisoners hadn't moved, but their demeanor had morphed from resigned to tense. The cadence of the vessel's rolling and pitching had changed. The *Nourakrina* was no longer just making way. She was maneuvering. That could only mean they were approaching the platform.

The two guards came simultaneously alert, as if they had heard something through their earpieces. They leveled their Kalashnikovs at the captives. One opened the compartment door.

The English speaking terrorist made a clumsy entrance. He wore a bulky flotation vest and carried two more. He handed one to each of the guards and took one of the Kalashnikovs to watch the prisoners so his men could fasten themselves into the vests. He emitted curt foreign syllables to hurry them along.

"All on deck," he ordered as soon as they were done.

Childers used the arms of his chair to push himself to his feet. His first steps were experimental, not taking him anywhere but just finding a way to stay upright with the floor rolling under him. One of the guards prodded him with the muzzle of an assault rifle. Tentative steps took him toward the door.

Corrigan, the four surviving crewmen, Childers and Flores were herded out. They moved along the gangway by fits and starts, prodded by the terrorists' weapons. Childers needed both hands on the gangway railing to maintain his balance.

Wind howling through an open hatchway ahead brought dampness and chill. Beyond the hatchway was the foredeck of the vessel. It was early afternoon by Childers' watch, but the deck lights were on in the gloom of the storm. Rain came in sheets, broken regularly when the ocean rose in huge waves and sent spray over the cargo containers lashed to the deck. Water sluiced among the deck fixtures on the pitching metal surface. The lead crewman stopped at the hatchway and yelled something over his shoulder at Corrigan. Childers pulled himself forward along the rail to catch the conversation.

The crewman was one of the South Asians. "We can not dock in this weather!"

A murmur of agreement rose from the other crewmen. This was the wrong time for them to rebel. Once they docked, most of the terrorists would abandon the vessel to seize the platform and the odds would shift in favor of the crew. Childers clung to the rail, frustrated and hoping Corrigan could keep his men in line.

The English speaking terrorist ordered Corrigan to get his men to their stations to prepare for docking.

"We'll need flotation vests," Corrigan said.

"Not enough for all."

"There are more in lockers below decks."

"What good does it do?"

"In this storm, any one of us could go overboard."

"Then you are no use. What does it matter if you float?"

"No jackets, no work," Corrigan retorted.

The terrorist put the muzzle of an automatic pistol under Corrigan's chin.

"Do as I say."

"Shoot and be damned," Corrigan said. "One round will warn the entire platform you're coming."

"There are other ways," the man said.

"None of them will get you docked," Corrigan said.

He spoke quietly and let the violence of the storm and the expressions of his men make his point. The routine would have to be performed in heavy seas by a recalcitrant crew. Loss of the supervising deck officer could doom the effort.

"Show me," the terrorist ordered and poked the muzzle of his pistol into Corrigan's ribs.

Corrigan led him back along the gangway and through an interior hatchway out of sight. The message to his crewmen was clear. For a brief window of time, he was in control. What he intended to do with that control was not at all clear.

Flores had taken advantage of the distraction to move close to Childers.

"I'll need to leave you," she said quietly.

"What for?"

"You'll be all right. I just need to do something."

"Can I help?" he asked.

"I'll need to slip away without being noticed. If you see me go, don't--"

A terrorist separated them with the muzzle of his assault rifle. A few words snarled in Arabic were probably meant to silence them. They underscored the tension in the young man's features. The moment he had been trained and indoctrinated for was close at hand. He was as frightened as anyone on the vessel. Childers avoided eye contact to keep from spooking him further.

Corrigan returned with an armload of flotation vests. Childers was handed one. He was unfamiliar with the fasteners and had to watch the crewmen to see how to put it on. Cold fingers didn't help. He had to release the railing and use both hands.

The sudden jolt of a wave threw him against the bulkhead. He went down hard and finished the job sitting on the metal floor of the gangway. A terrorist prodded him with a gun muzzle. He struggled to his feet and craned for a look out the hatchway.

The platform hove into view. Seen from the approaching helicopter it had been a small and isolated outpost in an endless ocean. Coming in at sea level the structure towered into an angry sky, too vast to be fully visible through the hatchway, s soulless mass of imposing steel with the froth of a roiling ocean coursing around one of the great flotation columns that supported it.

The docking area was visible beyond the stacks of cargo containers. The vessel began to turn, coming up to parallel the mooring. Pitching decreased in the lee of the platform, but the gargantuan structure loomed over them, rising and falling with every swell, like some drunken giant threatening to crush the *Nourakrina* with its next heedless lurch.

Childers was prodded out onto the foredeck with Flores, Corrigan and the crew. Wind came in powerful gusts, cuffing and threatening to topple him. Rain stung his exposed skin like needles. He used a hand to shield his face, squinting to see through the fog and water on his glasses.

Some of the crew already stood at stations by the rail, hanging on to keep their balance. Corrigan ordered the rest of his men to their stations. They moved cautiously and reluctantly out across the slippery deck. One of the terrorists followed them, doing his best to keep his assault rifle hidden under his raincoat.

The remaining terrorists gathered in the shelter of the vessel's superstructure, their weapons concealed under their coats, their visitor passes clearly visible. Eight of them formed a phalanx ahead of two others. The two had an oriental rather than Semitic look, and as Corrigan had suggested, did not seem any more accustomed than Childers to the heavy rolling of the vessel. He braced himself against an out of the way section of bulkhead to stay erect.

The assault force paid him scant attention; young men alone with their last personal thoughts before plunging into the unknown and the inevitable. Impact announced their contact with the platform and took Childers off his feet. He pulled himself back to a standing position.

Flores was nowhere to be seen. Childers counted eleven terrorists in view. If Corrigan's tally of twelve was accurate, that left one unaccounted for. He would be responsible for securing the bridge. That would be Flores target. The radios were there. She had been trained as part of a team, and her first instinct would be to call for help. It would be a pointless exercise in bravery. Even if she prevailed over the terrorist, help would not arrive in time.

Corrigan now had control of the full deck crew, but Childers doubted he could turn that to advantage against the terrorists. Seen from a safe elevation on the platform, the docking procedure had been an interesting bit of choreography. At deck level it was a wrestling match with sodden hawsers, a desperate struggle against violent weather. Every man was essential to the task. Only Childers remained free to move.

The terrorist near the railing would be the only one left on deck when the others swarmed onto the platform. Childers identified a sequence of deck fixtures and cables he could use as handholds to reach the man. Until the main terrorist force moved, there was nothing he could do but try to keep a lid on his nerves.

The *Nourakrina* groaned like something alive as it heaved on the gale and shuddered every time it slammed against the docking platform. It was an open question how much pounding the heavily laden vessel could take before it began to come apart. It seemed an eternity before the vessel was lashed against the platform's bumpers. The terrorists surged forward as a group, making their slippery and uncertain move toward the railing and the platform ladders. Childers brought up the rear, unnoticed in the eagerness of the moment.

The storm provided cover, but little else to compensate for the grief the slick deck and slicker metal of the fixtures caused him. He lost his footing and his grip and had to fight his way back to his feet. Wind made eerie noises in the steel cabling, like mocking laughter. He was a frail old man lost in the fantasies of his youth. He had no weapon and no allies. He was struggling through a storm to attack an armed zealot.

Through the blur of rain on his glasses he was able to make out the assault force climbing over the deck railing and starting up metal ladders to reach the platform dock. The single terrorist remaining on the deck of the vessel divided his attention between watching the crew and the progress of his comrades trying to gain the platform dock. Childers could see none of what transpired on the platform. He stayed low, closing on his quarry.

The terrorist stood gripping the rail to maintain his balance. It looked possible to grab a leg and tip him over the side into the narrow gap between the vessel and the platform. Even so, Childers was likely to slip on the wet deck and wind up in the ocean himself. His vest would keep him afloat, but hypothermia would kill him even if he weren't crushed against the vessel or the platform. He hadn't come this far to quit.

A sudden blast of wind stopped Childers' progress and left him fighting to hold his ground. The wind vanished as suddenly as it had arisen, and his struggles sent him stumbling forward.

The movement was enough to catch the terrorist's eye. He brought the Kalashnikov out from under his coat. Off balance and exposed all Childers could do was lunge at the man.

Chapter 29

$\mathcal{V}$ALENTINA FLORES SAT SHIVERING IN a corner. Her effort to slip quietly onto the bridge had gone as badly as everything else. A powerful gust of wind caught the door just as she cracked it for a peek inside, slamming it open and dragging her in with it. A terrorist stood not ten feet away. He leveled a Kalashnikov at her. There was nothing she could do but raise her hands, plop her butt on the floor and hope the fact that she looked like a drowned rat would make her seem like just a harmless hostage.

It was probably the terrorists' need for stealth that saved her. A helpless woman wasn't worth the risk of a gunshot that could alert the platform to the impending danger. The terrorist glanced out to be sure Flores was alone and then secured the door.

The bridge was wide and claustrophobically shallow. LEDs on the communications panel verified that the equipment was still live. That raised the hope of getting a message out. It also raised the risk level. The terrorist left to watch over that sort of capability wouldn't be some juvenile indoctrinee. He would have to be fluent in English and familiar with the hardware. He was a few years older than the guards in the crew lounge and seemed surer of himself. In place of a simple earpiece he wore a two way Bluetooth. Flores would have to snatch that away to isolate him.

It wouldn't be easy. The storm coat and the floatation vest that concealed her automatic also stood in the way of retrieving it. Wet clothing clung at every move she made. She could move only when the terrorist was looking elsewhere and no move could be energetic enough to attract attention. She had only a limited time to act. She knew from the faces of the crew members in the lounge that mutiny was possible.

Besides Flores and the terrorist there were only two others on the bridge. A seaman held the wheel. Ruddy color in his sagging jowls and a bulbous, veined nose gave him the look of a cherub gone to seed. The remaining man would be Captain Peterson. He was a fattish sort who might be mistaken for an accountant without his officer's cap. The cast of his features was puritanical, uncompromising. He peered through the windows, watching the activity on the deck below.

The windows were slanted inward, offering a view clear of rain. Flores was sitting too low to take advantage of it. She doubted that Childers would instigate anything. He had talked a good fight but at his age both his strength and his nerve would fall victim to the savage weather. Captain Peterson had probably ordered the ship's company to obey the terrorists to maintain control and minimize risk, but once word of the young sailor's death and callous disposal spread, all bets would be off. The question was how Peterson would react if the situation went south on him. She cringed at the thought that she might have to shoot him to gain control of the radios.

Conscience no longer mattered. The lives of everyone on the platform and the future of a whole section of the coast might depend on the military getting precise and timely information. The radio call had to go out. The terrorist's attention was riveted out the window and Flores guessed the boarding party was moving. She released the catches on her life vest and unzipped her coat.

A quick burst of automatic gunfire came from the deck below, shattering the rhythm of the storm. The terrorist moved toward the door. Peterson stepped to block him, a futile and dangerous effort to protect the crew. The terrorist pushed Peterson against the control panel and brought his rifle up to bear. The terrorist's back was to Flores. She jerked the pistol out from under her coat.

The automatic bucked in her grip. The bullet hammered through the terrorist's raincoat between his shoulder blades. He staggered, but didn't go down. He turned on Flores. Her second shot took the man in the chest. It shook him visibly but he was a soldier of God and he wasn't giving up. The seaman abandoned the wheel and moved to tackle him. The seaman was at best the veteran of a few bar fights. The terrorist had been trained. A rifle butt to the side of the seaman's head put him on his knees, stunned. Flores focused on the pistol's sights.

The Glock bucked for the third time. The terrorist's head jerked and the left rear of his skull tore away from the force of the bullet. He crumpled and lay still. Flores scrambled across the floor and grabbed the rifle. She couldn't free it from the sling under the man's coat and she couldn't waste time wrestling with it. She jerked out the magazine and discarded it.

Her last shot had shattered the window pane behind the terrorist. Wind blew in and rain swirled in the shallow space. She got her feet under her and rose to peer out. She could discern only vague shapes moving on the deck below. There were figures on the drilling platform. Flashes of red erupted from there. She ducked as the remaining windows shattered under a burst of automatic gunfire.

There was a thud and the vessel rolled, hurling her back into her corner. The impact sent her surroundings spinning. She shook her head and tried to focus on something beyond the strands of wet hair dangling in front of her eyes.

The vessel began pitching as well as rolling. They had apparently come loose from the platform. There was nothing to keep them from being slammed against the mooring. Peterson grabbed the wheel and reached for something on the control console. The diesels throbbed through the metal superstructure. The vessel heaved, thudded against the platform and then ricocheted away. Flores hunkered in her corner, wondering how long she could last in the cold Pacific with only a life jacket.

Wind blew the door open. Childers came in, half walking and half supported by the Korean sailor from the crew lounge. The crewman released him and he sagged down into a sitting position against a bulkhead. The crewman went to Peterson.

"Captain, Sir, Mr. Corrigan tell you deck secure. No more man with gun. We throw him overboard."

"On whose authority?" Peterson's voice was taut, angry.

"Mr. Corrigan, Sir. First Officer. We are fighting with man. Can't get his gun away. Mr. Corrigan say throw him overboard. Orders, Sir. Mr. Corrigan. First Officer."

"Mr. Corrigan to the bridge," Peterson snapped.

The Korean hustled out. The sailor who had manned the wheel got up slowly from the floor. Peterson watched him catch the console for support and then test his balance.

"Are you all right, lad?"

"Yes, Sir."

The man didn't sound overly sure of himself. Corrigan came in. Peterson glared at him.

"You had one of the pirates thrown overboard."

"Him or us, Captain," Corrigan said.

"Why did you attack him?"

"Him or us. They killed Dexter. Shot him for nothing more than trying to bum a smoke. Threw him overboard like so much trash."

Peterson winced but his glare remained steady. "Weren't you told they've placed a scuttling charge on board?"

"No." Corrigan's surprise looked genuine.

"They can blow it remotely any time."

It was the first Flores had heard of any bomb. She forced herself to her feet, finding her balance on the rolling surface.

"Captain," she said, "we need to get a radio call to the military. They can provide guidance to search for and disarm any munition."

Peterson turned his cold glare on her. "I've had more than enough of being threatened by people waving guns. You'll put that pistol away or I'll have it taken by force."

Flores hadn't realized she was still holding her Glock. She holstered it and took out her identification.

"My name is Valentina Flores. I'm a Deputy US..."

"There'll be no search," Peterson said. "We may lose the *Nourakrina* but we'll risk no more crew. Mr. Corrigan."

"Aye, Sir."

"Get a party together and close all the watertight hatches. We'll seal off any damage as much as possible and take the *Nourakrina* as far as she'll go. I want men standing by to launch lifeboats on command. Alert the engine room crew and make sure they all have floatation gear."

"Aye, Sir."

Corrigan was gone as quickly as he had come, probably glad to escape Peterson's wrath. Flores made her way to the control console. The pitching and tossing were too much and she had to grab the console for support.

"Captain, we do need to get a radio call out."

"There's a procedure for these things. An order they're done in. Operate. Navigate. Communicate."

"I can make the call," Flores said. "Do you have an emergency military channel?"

"Would know who you were talking to? Recognize a voice?"

"The right channel will get us to the people we need to reach."

Peterson shook his head. "Do you think you're dealing with fools? The pirate running communication during the trip out has forgotten more than I'll ever know about marine radio. If he left us an open channel, it'll be for his purposes. Not ours."

Peterson was right. She had no means of authentication. The call could be shunted to a radio that belonged to the terrorists. They could intercept any request for help.

"Well, we can't just do nothing," she said.

"I'll call on the regular channel. Get someone I know. Have the message relayed on a secure line."

"Then do it."

"Miss, that adrenaline is draining out of you. I can see it in your eyes. You'll have the shakes in a minute. You better sit down before you fall down."

Flores' legs began to tremble. She moved awkwardly to Childers and slumped down beside him. She couldn't believe she had lost it physically. She had never felt so helpless. She wondered if the same fate had overtaken Childers, or if it was something worse.

"Are you all right?" she asked.

"I hurt in a lot of places, but I don't think anything's broken."

"We'll get you checked out as soon as we dock."

Who was she kidding? They were in the middle of nowhere on a boat that could blow sky high any second and no one anywhere else had a clue they were in trouble.

"You did a good job," he said.

"Yeah. Right." That's what her mother used to tell her when she cleaned her room.

"No, don't blow it off. You need to understand that you did the right thing. It may not matter this minute, but later, when the nightmares come, you need to understand that you did the best anyone could possibly have done in the situation."

Best anyone could have done in the situation. Christ, she had bungled what few things she had been trained to do, and really flopped after that. She watched two sailors drag the dead terrorist out, leaving a blood stain that she might never wash out of her mind.

Nothing she had been taught had prepared her for this. Childers may have been right about nightmares coming, but all she felt now was an overwhelming urge to kick the crap out of the morons who wrote the Marshals Service training syllabus. She was on her own, and she needed to get back in the game.

"Do you still have your cell phone?" she asked Childers.

"It's in the car charger."

"Captain Peterson?" she yelled over the howl of wind through the broken glass.

"What?" he snapped without taking his attention from the helm.

"Cell phone?"

"Broken and thrown overboard. Just like yours. For the last time, these people are not fools."

Flores cursed under her breath. Peterson was right. This was more than just a bunch of crazies with a wild hair up their asses. Her partner was following an Escalade that was somehow connected with the raid on the platform. She needed to know where it had gone and who else was involved. If she got another chance, she would do it right. Gather information. Assess the situation. Formulate a plan. Obtain adequate resources. Brief and supervise. No more screw-ups.

Chapter 30

PHILIP LINFIELD HAD BUILT A career on his ability to handle difficult people and developing situations. The process was no different than intermission during a concert. New music might be coming up on the racks, but the instruments and the players remained the same. It would be his role as conductor to manage the change of score and orchestrate a satisfactory performance. He needed to regain the initiative and assert control.

"I am sure Your Highness' plan was well conceived and undertaken with the best of intentions," Linfield said. "It might have been workable if you hadn't blown up that Van Wyck fellow."

"Who?"

"Spenser Van Wyck. International banking."

"I don't know the name."

It was a matter-of-fact statement with an unsettling ring of truth. Linfield wasn't sure what to make of it.

"He died in that condominium bombing a few weeks ago."

"I don't blow people up, Mr. Linfield. You are thinking of a misguided crop of jihadists. When I am ready to move, I will have effective control over the world's petroleum recovery. Governments will have no choice but to obey me, and that obedience will give me leverage far beyond infrastructure and production. This is a sophisticated operation. No more violence is employed than is absolutely necessary."

Elmer hadn't specifically accused The Prince of involvement in the bombing, and it probably didn't matter whether he was or not.

"Van Wyck discovered your plan," Linfield said. "He came to San Francisco to thwart it. The bombing that killed him claimed a dozen lives. That will bring the Government down on you, culpable or not."

The Prince considered Linfield while he chewed a piece of lamb. "You are suggesting that I could become collateral damage as a result of some unidentified third party's actions?"

"That can be avoided, Your Highness."

"Can it indeed?"

"Simply abort your plan," Linfield said.

"Abort?"

"United States law requires both an overt act and criminal intent for a conviction. As long as you stop short of the act, you will be perfectly safe."

"The project has already consumed hundreds of millions of dollars. You cannot possibly expect me to abort based on some threat that is no more than vapor."

"Van Wyck's widow is making a lot of noise," Linfield said. "Right or wrong, she does have access to the corridors of power."

"American women," The Prince said, "are taken no more seriously than those in what you would patronizingly call the third world."

"Can you afford to gamble?" Linfield asked.

"The die is already cast. My forces have taken the platform."

Linfield was stunned. Months of work and commitment, millions of his own resources, his dreams for the future, wiped out in a single, senseless act of violence.

"What sort of barbarian are you?" Linfield demanded.

The Prince's face darkened. "Any barbarism is your doing. There is no way to approach an oil platform in mid-ocean without being seen. Had you met my schedule for the Hollister acquisition, had we been able to act before the worst of the weather set in, we could have used subterfuge to gain access to the platform and taken control by a simple show of force. Thanks to your delay, my men were compelled to commandeer Hollister's supply boat in the harbor. There was a mutiny during docking with the platform. Two of Allah's finest soldiers have been martyred. The supply boat cut itself adrift from the platform and is now at the mercy of the elements."

Linfield felt his tongue moisten his lips, an involuntary show of nerves that he could ill afford. He needed to keep his head, find an edge.

"Then your men are trapped on the platform," he said.

"A speedboat is enroute to evacuate them."

"You're finished," Linfield said. "The military will be on you."

"There are times when we have only faith in God to sustain us. I would point out that the storm could not exist without the will of Allah. As sorely as it may test the faithful, it will also protect them from his enemies. But you would only scoff."

"A single victory is hardly a conquest," Linfield observed. "Hackers may do considerable mischief, but the sophistication required to construct the code you describe rests only in technologically advanced countries and is tightly held at the highest government and corporate levels."

"As a young man," The Prince said, "I learned to my great delight that any woman's legs could be separated by the judicious application of treasure. As I matured, I learned to apply the same method when it came to separating the talent I needed from its existing loyalties."

"Then why not bribe someone to install your code?" Linfield asked. "Why risk invading the platform?"

"The option was given careful consideration, but incursion was deemed the lesser risk. Anyone prepared to betray his masters for my money might betray me for a larger sum. The entire plan hinges on successful insertion of the code. The job could be entrusted to only the most dedicated and loyal of men."

The fellow sounded quite mad. However bad the circumstances, panic wouldn't help. Linfield needed to remain calm and try to put the conversation back on a rational footing.

"Whatever damage you manage to inflict," Linfield said, "I think you will find American resistance will stiffen in proportion. With all due respect to Your Highness' beneficence, Americans don't like to be ruled. It offends their sense of equality and fairness."

"Equality and fairness?" The Prince studied Linfield with mocking eyes. "A nation that squanders billions on drugs, alcohol and wagering in a world where hundreds of millions of people subsist on less than a dollar a day has little to offer in the way of equality and fairness. If your countrymen had to face the reality of equality and fairness, they would fall on their knees and beg for a despot to save them."

More pointless rhetoric. Best to stick to practical matters.

"Even so, you will never be able to see your plan to conclusion," Linfield said. "You are familiar with the documents. You know that I have operational control of Hollister."

"You have control because you are agent of record for the parent company. That is easily changed if you wish to select a proxy. It would have to be changed in the event of your departure."

"I have no intention of leaving," Linfield retorted.

The Prince settled himself in the armchair. "What will you have to remain for? Expansion funding will not be forthcoming if you do not meet my terms."

"Other sources can be found," Linfield said. "Finance is my forte."

"I have no time to haggle."

"I will not be party to a criminal conspiracy. Particularly not one that is known to the Government."

"The American security apparatus is paranoid in the wake of 9/11," The Prince said. "The Government would not have allowed my plan to progress as far as it has if they had even an inkling of its existence. No, Mr. Linfield, I think we may be assured of their ignorance"

"I do not intend to either step aside or be thrust aside," Linfield said.

"That decision, Mr. Linfield, I have already made. The machinery of execution is immediately at hand. A stormy afternoon. A dangerous road. Two executives perpetually in a hurry."

This lunatic was prepared to murder them.

"My people have been in contact with Mr. Quist," The Prince went on. "They characterize him as a cooperative chap who asks few questions beyond how his own interests will be served. He should provide satisfactory camouflage."

That was why Quist had dropped his opposition to the buyout. The weasel had been promised control of the reconstituted Hollister firm.

"You won't get away with it," Linfield said.

"We are already there," The Prince said, skewering a piece of lamb on his fork. "Thanks in no small part to your sterling efforts."

He chewed slowly and carefully while he considered Linfield.

"You have put together an impressive organization and an inviting smorgasbord of contacts. I really would like to have you along on this little adventure. The rewards will be handsome, the risks minuscule and you will have the satisfaction of being on the winning side."

"You have no chance."

The Prince wiped his mouth and stood. "I have tolerated your foolish prattle in the hope I could bring you on board. If that is not to be, there is no more point. As a precaution I will need to be out of US Airspace when final resolution is made."

The Prince gave instructions to the thugs in Arabic, then smiled down at Linfield and Montgomery.

"You will have a few hours for any final thoughts you may have. Then you will have the honor of becoming among the first casualties in the final victory of Islam over the forces of evil."

The Prince swept out of the room.

Linfield patted his lips with a napkin and stood. Montgomery came out of his chair. He was tall and strapping, though not as thickly muscled as the two shorter thugs who moved to flank him.

"Let's just get out of here," he said. "They can't stop us."

One of the thugs hit him behind the ear with a blackjack. He sagged to his knees, not quite unconscious and struggling not to fall. His hands were bound behind him with duct tape. Linfield was pushed down beside him and bound similarly. A panicky glance from Montgomery told Linfield the fellow had recovered at least some mental faculty. Linfield spoke quietly.

"Best to wait. These fellows certainly have firearms."

Montgomery shook off the remainder of his visible grogginess but couldn't manage words.

"It is imperative that at least one of us escape," Linfield said. "We are the only two who know the full scope of the fellow's plan."

"H-how?" Montgomery asked.

"These buffoons have made a tactical blunder. There is no vehicle access to the bungalow. They will have to unbind us when they walk us to the parking lot. They won't dare use force once we are outside in public. We'll make our move then."

185

Linfield bridled at the indignity of having duct tape slapped over his mouth, but he did not struggle. That would come later, when the odds favored them and surprise could be achieved. Their captors would have to take them along a footpath in full view of flanking bungalows and the parking lot. Swift kicks to the shins. A dash for liberty. If he and Montgomery split up, at least one of them would be able to raise enough ruckus to bring help. The trick would be communicating the remainder of his strategy to Montgomery.

Chapter 31

*E*ARL CHILDERS HUDDLED IN THE lee of the superstructure with Flores and the crewmen responsible to launch the nearby lifeboat. Conversation was impossible over the noise of the storm. A distant throb of helicopter rotors was gone as quickly as it came. There seemed no end to the monotony of the ocean. Childers lost track of time. At some point a stirring among the crew caught his ear.

Multicolored strobes were visible against the clouds. A Coast Guard cutter materialized out of the storm. The boarding party arrived with a German shepherd, probably trained to detect explosives. An officer went with Corrigan to the bridge while the others stood by, as if time had been put on hold and the scuttling charge wouldn't dare blow while the niceties of maritime protocol were being observed.

The trip to a waiting cutter was a shivering, stomach churning ride in the small boat that had brought the boarding party. Childers and Flores were taken to the ward room. A medical corpsman came to check their vital signs. Flores used her badge to borrow his cell phone. Childers could hear only her side of the conversation.

"Hey, Ed, it's me. Do you still have that Escalade?…Yes, I know the surveillance was scheduled to be discontinued…What was the last location?…Did you get a look at the driver?…Any passengers?…Nothing is wrong, Ed. I'm just trying to connect the dots…Okay, thanks."

She returned the phone and asked the Corpsman what had happened on the platform. He knew nothing beyond the cutter's assignment: intercept the *Nourakrina* before it reached the harbor, clear it of explosives and return the occupants to port. A tug would take the vessel to investigative impound. Flores thanked him and he left.

"Are you okay to drive?" she asked Childers.

"Where?"

"Down the coast."

"Won't the authorities want to talk to us?" he asked. "Three people were killed."

"There's no rush. They're not going to get any deader."

As soon as they docked Flores used her badge to get them both off the cutter. The walk to the Honda left both of them soaked. Flores didn't seem to care.

"You're driving," she said as soon as they were underway, "because we need to talk."

"What is my status?" Childers asked.

"About the GF," Flores said.

"Excuse me?"

"Girl friend. Pilar Monterosa. Ring any bells?"

Flores' surveillance would have seen Pilar come and go. "I'm pretty sure that was a limited time offer," he said. "One to a customer. Expired by now."

"She was involved in what happened today."

Childers was sure Pilar was playing a bigger game than was obvious from the Hollister buyout, but he couldn't reconcile the smart, elegant woman with the violence on the *Nourakrina*.

"Involved how?" he asked.

"She knew that the platform would be raided. Several weeks ago. Just after she saw you. I need to know everything you know about her, and I need to know right now."

"If I'm under arrest, I think we'll go to your office and I'll call my attorney."

"Keep driving."

"You may have the badge and the gun," Childers said, "but I have the accelerator and if I punch this thing up to a hundred and a quarter we'll attract a lot of attention and a lot of police."

"Just trust me," she said. "It's important"

"Trust you? If you people knew Pilar knew about the raid, then you must have known too. Why didn't you pre-empt it?"

"I didn't start putting the pieces together until it was too late," Flores said.

"Spenser Van Wyck tried to warn you people. I tried to warn Levi Weiss. Nobody in Government wanted to listen."

"I'm in Government. I'm listening."

Childers repeated Pilar's autobiography as Ray Parker had sketched it for him.

"A maroon Escalade has been following Monterosa." Flores said. "That same car was at the harbor this morning. My partner followed it. It took a Chinese woman to a motel down the coast."

Childers recalled the Chinaman and the attempt on his life. The answers to who wanted him dead and why might lie at the end of Flores' quest. This might be his only chance to find them.

Approaching dusk added to the gloom of the storm to cut visibility to not much more than the reach of the headlights. Discreet neon marked the turnoff to Castillo del Mar. There was a soft glow from enough windows in the main building to testify to respectable occupancy.

"Slow cruise through the parking lot," Flores instructed.

Elevated sodium lamps raised highlights in row after row of vehicles. Bits of light in the adjoining shrubbery suggested outbuildings. The Honda's headlights swept past two young men with glowing cigarettes lounging beside a motorcycle under a bit of roof overhang. Probably just staff forced to take their break outside by California's welter of anti-smoking ordinances.

"There," Flores said.

The vehicle she indicated was an economy sedan parked at the end of an asphalt path leading back into the shrubbery.

"That's white," Childers said. "And I'm pretty sure it's not an Escalade."

"I've ridden in that car. It was rented by Philip Linfield's company."

Flores cracked the passenger door.

"Let me out here. Drive straight home. Call the Marshals Service. Give them your location."

She got out into the rain, shut the door and made a dash for the sedan. The two men by the motorcycle watched her peer into the car, but it didn't seem to amount to anything beyond idle curiosity. Childers had been shown the door. He rolled on through the lot and back to the access road.

Another vehicle was coming up as Childers started down. Its high beams blinded him briefly, but as they passed each other he recognized it as a maroon Escalade.

Screw it. It wasn't his problem. He had put in his years. He was entitled to a quiet retirement. The Government couldn't ignore the situation any longer. They would have to earn their salaries and get to the bottom of it. He got as far as the bottom of the access road before he said, "shit," killed the vehicle lights, turned around and crept back up to the parking lot.

Doreen Munn answered his cell phone call on the second ring. "Earl, where are you?"

"A place called Castillo del Mar." Childers let the Honda drift to a stop so he would show no brake lights.

"The authorities are looking all over for you."

"They are also missing a Deputy US Marshal."

"Do you know where Flores is?"

"She's here," Childers said, even though he had lost sight of her in the storm.

"You need to come in now. Bring Flores with you."

"Doreen, get real. She's the police official. Not me."

"Talk to her. Tell her to call in."

"I don't think she's in a listening mood. She has information no one else seems to have, and I'm afraid she's getting dangerously far ahead of whatever investigation these people have going."

"Then she needs to check in."

"It's not that simple. She shot someone today, and she has no experience dealing with combat stress. The Feds need to get someone out here to get a leash on her before things get out of hand. Can you call your buddy Tremaine?"

"What about you?" Munn asked.

"Tell them you'll surrender me as soon as we've talked."

Childers cut the connection.

A man had emerged from the shrubbery next to the white economy sedan. He wore the same style of raincoat as the terrorists on the *Nourakrina*. He looked left and right and waved an arm. A motorcycle engine caught and revved briefly. Childers had lost track of the Escalade. Flores was nowhere to be seen. He killed the engine and bailed out of the Honda, shutting the door quickly and quietly to minimize the light and noise associated with his movement.

Crouched between two parked cars Childers had a clear view of the sedan and the path beyond it. Still no sign of Flores. The motorcycle idled away from the main building, lights out, two men straddling it. The man beside the sedan unbuttoned his coat to reveal a Kalashnikov slung beneath. Childers went back, retrieved the Winchester from the Honda and returned to cover between the two cars, using a sleeve to wipe water from his glasses.

A group of four men was moving along the path toward the sedan. Only Philip Linfield was familiar, and he looked oddly out of sorts. He had neither a hat nor an umbrella. Misaligned buttons left his raincoat askew. Behind him was younger and taller man, similarly dressed. Both rubbed their wrists and walked a bit clumsily, as if circulation was just returning to their legs. Beside each was a man holding him by the arm hustling him along. Childers braced his rifle across the trunk of the nearest car.

Linfield stomped on the foot of the man holding him, twisted his arm free. Linfield's companion kicked the man holding him and drove a shoulder into the man, knocking him back off balance. Linfield and his companion separated, fleeing in different directions.

The motorcycle sprinted from its cover. The man on the back raised a shoulder weapon, firing first at Linfield and then on his companion. Childers aligned the Winchester's sights as best he could through rain blurred glasses.

The range was short and his shot took the man on the rear of the motorcycle in the back, blew through him and hit the driver. A muscle spasm sent the motorcycle out of control, spilling both men, sending them sliding and rolling. The shot had given away Childers' position. He ducked behind the car.

A burst of automatic gunfire shattered the windows and showered him with bits of glass. Flores' voice came over the storm.

"Bill, stay down."

A flurry of gunfire followed. Childers levered a fresh cartridge into the chamber of the Winchester. He crept along the side of the car and raised his head cautiously to peer over the hood.

Linfield's dash for freedom had carried him as far as a hedge. The shrubbery was thick and about four feet high and he lay against it as limp as a piece of wind-blown trash. The man who held Linfield's arm and pursued him when he ran lay partially visible, face down in a puddle on the asphalt path.

Linfield's companion was down but still struggling feebly to move. The man who had held him was backing away from him, shambling and shuffling in the general direction of the sedan. He fired a pistol into the storm, one random shot and then another. Mist danced briefly in a pencil-thin shaft of intense red light. The man stopped quite suddenly and collapsed in a boneless heap.

Flores broke from the cover of a tree. She ran to Linfield's companion. The man Childers had seen unlock the sedan rose and brought up an abbreviated shoulder weapon. Before Childers could bring the Winchester to bear a red dot appeared on the back of the man's head. His head jerked and he collapsed. Childers ducked between cars.

There were no more shots. Childers rose cautiously.

Only Flores showed life, crouched over Linfield's companion. Sirens howled in the distance. The adrenaline that had sustained Childers was draining away. He was trembling when reached the Honda. He was on the highway before the police arrived, passing them going in the other direction, just another motorist making his way home in the late evening traffic.

The raid on the oil drilling platform was the top news story on television. Terrorists had seized control of the platform. Navy Seals had reacted quickly and retaken the facility before any damage could be done. The terrorists had escaped in a waiting speedboat. A search was underway. Government spokespeople were full of assurances that no oil had been leaked, and that appropriate monitoring was in place.

A breaking news report had film from a shooting south of the city. A med-evac helicopter was shown landing. Details were promised. Childers shut it off.

Hunger overrode exhaustion and demanded dinner. Afterward he loaded the dishwasher and ran a bore snake through the Winchester. An old man with an antique rifle and a young woman with a pistol had been no match for five armed terrorists. Someone had come to the motel parking lot with a list of people to kill. He and Flores were alive because they weren't expected and weren't on the list.

Childers sat in the dimness of his recreation room with an iced Coca Cola, staring at Uncle Scrooge. The idea beginning to nag at him was as strange as anything a comic book artist could dream up.

Chapter 32

*V*ALENTINA FLORES HAD USED HER badge to board the med-evac helicopter. The airframe shuddered as the machine rose into the storm. Flores held one of Bill's hands in both of hers, trying to rub some warmth into it. Behind her she could hear the medical team struggling to resuscitate Philip Linfield. When they landed at the hospital, The ER staff worked for twenty frantic minutes before they gave up and declared Linfield dead. Bill survived surgery, as much as the doctors dared do in his condition. He died in the ICU at six minutes past one in the morning, without ever regaining consciousness.

After that, events were a blur. Flores was placed on paid administrative leave, her service automatic confiscated for processing. There would be a shooting review. She was to discuss events with no one in or out of the Marshals Service. Communication between the Service and the FBI being what it was, Tremaine may not have been notified of that when she called and told Flores to bring Earl Childers to her office. Flores was beyond caring what the Marshals Service thought. She wanted answers.

Flores and Childers sat side by side, facing Tremaine across her desk. Tremaine was wearing glasses. They were stylish and probably expensive, but they couldn't hide the effect of too many hours with contacts in.

"I need to know why the two of you went to Castillo del Mar," Tremaine said very quietly and precisely.

"I need to know why Bill Montgomery was killed," Flores said.

It wasn't a tone she would normally take with an FBI supervisor, but this interview wasn't normal. She and Childers should be signing separate written statements; the statements should then be gone over line by line for inconsistencies. For some reason, Tremaine didn't want this conversation on the record.

"If I don't get an answer," Flores said, "I will get in front of the first television camera I can find and throw a public tantrum that will have every news organization in the country down on you."

"Tantrum?" Tremaine didn't quite smile.

"You sent me to follow a woman several weeks ago. When I reported back, I told you Fort Apache was a target. You did nothing. This is your girl friend, Mr. Childers. Pilar Monterosa."

"I can give you the name of a reporter for the *Wall Street Journal*," Childers said. "She is half a step behind this. If she can interview you, she will figure it out."

Tremaine rippled impatient fingers on her desk blotter. Her nails still held residue of the dark varnish that had helped transform her into an Argentine prostitute.

"I need to know why the two of you went to Castillo del Mar," she repeated.

Both Tremaine and Childers seemed to know more than Flores did. Cooperation might get her more than confrontation. She could always make a scene later.

"The Escalade I reported the night I followed the Monterosa woman turned up again when Mr. Childers went to the Harbor. From there it led us to Castillo del Mar."

"Why did you go to the harbor?" Tremaine asked Childers.

"For the same reason Spenser Van Wyck came to San Francisco. I thought I had stumbled onto a Middle Eastern scheme to infect Hollister's control system with a computer virus. It wasn't until last night that I realized the scheme must have been sponsored by the US Government."

Tremaine's fingers were suddenly still, and Flores knew she had struck pay dirt.

"What led you to that conclusion?" Tremaine asked.

"The first clue was Pilar Monterossa," Childers said. "No one with her talent and connections should be working at Hollister. Her only possible motivation was US Citizenship. She was once well-placed in the British banking system, with access to world class players. She must have gotten wind of a scheme to infect commercial software and gone to the US Government with an offer to trade for cooperation."

"Speculation," Tremaine said.

"The Chinaman who paid to have me killed was real. So were the Orientals on the boat. No terror network has the resources to effectively wage cyber war. They must have scouted around for talent and attracted the attention of a government hostile to the US. That government provided the talent, probably in the guise of rogue programmers. Once the virus was in place, the terrorists could be pushed aside."

"You were accusing the US Government of sponsoring a terrorist act," Tremaine pointed out. "Now you say a government inimical to US interests sponsored the scheme."

"Both," Childers said. "For the US it was a major intelligence coup. Allowing the virus code to be installed would deliver the bad guys' blueprint for cyber war without them knowing we had it. All the Government had to do was entice them into a controlled situation. A sucker named Earl Childers gave them the opportunity."

"You don't lack for ego," Tremaine remarked.

Childers conceded the point with a meager smile. "I filed a fraud complaint in connection with Hollister. Hollister had software ripe for infiltration, so instead of the usual wrist-slap settlement the Justice Department assigned a frontline prosecutor and took the case to trial. That put Hollister in the news. Planted stories about the software put it on the terrorists' radar. It was a matter of time until they hooked up with a private equity firm to put their plan into action."

Flores felt her temper boil. "Did Philip Linfield know?"

"My impression was that he was in it for the money," Childers said, and glanced at Tremaine. "If the FBI was monitoring him, they may know more."

"If any of this were true," Tremaine said, "information would be released only on a need to know basis. I wouldn't have been told."

"You sent me to follow the Monterosa woman," Flores said, "so you would have independent confirmation that she was following the script, and that she was being followed, as she probably suspected. The man she met was a US military officer. She warned him that Fort Apache would be raided, and I warned you. Neither you nor he did anything to prevent what happened."

"Those charged with tactical implementation," Tremaine said, "would necessarily have acted on the instructions provided them."

"People were killed. In the Savannah bombing. On the boat. At Castillo Del Mar."

Tremaine removed her glasses and sank back into her chair. Age and fatigue lined her face.

"It was expected," she said, "when the operation was conceived, that the conspirators would rely on some combination of bribery and stealth to insert their virus. Subsequent information modified that expectation, but the risks appeared manageable. The platform crew could be replaced at the appropriate time by hand-picked military volunteers trained on a similar facility. Protection could be arranged for any endangered individuals. The one thing that wasn't anticipated was the hijacking of the supply boat."

Childers shifted uncomfortably in his chair. "Why protect me and not Van Wyck?"

"Mr. Van Wyck was told not to pursue the matter. He was dead before anyone realized he intended to disregard his instructions."

"He was just trying to do the right thing," Childers said.

"We all were," Flores said. Tears burned her eyes at the memory of holding Bill's hand in the helicopter.

Tremaine replaced her glasses. "I'm not sure either of you fully comprehend what is at stake. Malicious software can lie dormant for years and switch on without any action by those who launched it. It can disable emergency services, cause the manufacture of dangerously defective products, blow up petroleum facilities, poison food and water, make medical treatments lethal, devastate the electric power grid, discredit the banking system, ground airplanes, cause trains to collide and even turn our own military equipment against us.

"Once planted, it cannot be reliably detected. It can hide anywhere, masquerade as any program, and even move itself to another location in response to efforts to hunt it down. The only defense we have is to find it upon insertion. We are talking about world security, and since everyone benefits, everyone must be prepared to sacrifice if circumstances require it."

Flores recalled the endless hours she had spent on surveillance waiting for some two bit violator, day-dreaming about participating in a major national security operation. In her fantasies, she had always been the heroine. Never the goat.

"How badly did I mess things up?" she asked.

"That can't be changed," Tremaine said, and drew a snort from Childers.

"You clucks should be thanking us," he said.

"Excuse me? Clucks?"

"Your clever plan didn't fool a sick old man. It certainly wouldn't have fooled the experienced military people behind this. It was too simple. You made it too easy for them to execute. Real projects are complicated. Messy. Full of uncertainty. This one started to look real when Van Wyck got wind of the terrorists' intentions and the sponsors had to bomb the Savannah to eliminate him and the group he was putting together to expose the scheme. It looked even better when they failed to kill me and could do nothing but sit and sweat, waiting to learn whether Van Wyck had told me anything. Marshal Flores crashing the party at Castillo del Mar removed any chance the US Government was leading them on and left them believing the whole thing."

"I hope you are right about that last," Tremaine said.

"The Escalade showed up after Marshal Flores and I separated. The occupants did most of the effective shooting. They came prepared to silence anyone with direct knowledge of the virus, but they didn't shoot Marshal Flores or myself, which they could easily have done. They are satisfied and don't want to make any more waves."

"And just what do you intend to do about all this?" Tremaine asked.

"Keep my mouth shut," Childers said. "Like the other Hollister people who must know. I presume the reason I couldn't find either software engineer was that they were busy helping the Government shunt the virus onto a secure server, where the operations of the platform software could be mirrored so the bad guys won't know they aren't really connected."

"Marshal Flores?" Tremaine asked.

"Just tell me what I need to do to keep from screwing things up."

Tremaine handed her a padded envelope containing her service automatic. The FBI had assumed responsibility for her shooting review. She would be given a prepared statement to sign. The matter would be sealed under National Security.

"There is one thing you both need to know," Tremaine said. "The shooting at Castillo del Mar, combined with an earlier FBI raid in Oakland, will be presented to the media as resolution of the Savannah incident as an isolated act of terrorism. Neither of you will comment on that, publicly or privately. Is that clear?"

It was over. Just like that. The world depended on life continuing as it always had, as if nothing had happened. Tremaine thanked them for coming and walked them out to reception.

"How did you do in the Western Regionals?" Flores asked.

"We were second alternate couple for the finals. We wouldn't have danced even if I had been able to attend."

"At least it was a positive note to go out on."

"As a dancer, perhaps," Tremaine said. "Only Mr. Childers rides off into the sunset with a full wallet and no regrets."

"I ride off into surgery," Childers corrected. "My Doctor called this morning. My cancer is back. I check in to the hospital at 6:00 AM tomorrow to have a chemo port implanted. After that I am looking at six months of nasty side effects as a best case. Worst case, I better clean up as much of my personal bucket list as I can while I'm still on the right side of the grass."

The good guys had won. It was the kind of victory that might wind up in the history books someday, if anyone ever found out about it. Flores felt as empty of emotion as a scarecrow, riding down in the elevator with an old man facing a long fight with an unpredictable outcome.

"Cluster fuck," she muttered to herself.

"A butterfly flaps its wings in China," Childers said, "and if conditions are exactly right, sets off a chain reaction that sends a hurricane into the Caribbean. We are all blown on the gales of chance, and our best reaction is usually clumsy and costly."

"You are a success," Flores said. "You can afford philosophy."

"Success," Childers said, "is the progressive realization of a self determined, worthwhile goal. The success lies in the progress. Once you get where you're going, the progress stops and you're not succeeding any more. Anyone who actually achieves a goal is a loser who didn't aim high enough."

A smug old man who had it all figured out.

His words haunted her on the plane ride back to DC and her life, what was left of it. She knew now that Bill Montgomery would never have been part of that life. He was a catch and there had been plenty of chicks in his past. He had learned to play them for what he wanted. He had played her in the hope of getting any edge in the Hollister deal. She couldn't bring herself to hate him for it. He hadn't deserved to die, but he wasn't coming back.

Maybe the old coot had it right. It sounded back-assward, but the goals she had reached seemed empty as soon as she achieved them and the ones snatched away by circumstance left her frustrated and confronting her own short-comings. She needed to re-think her whole fucking future. Throw out all the shit she had been conditioned to believe. Figure out what worked for her and to hell with what anyone else thought about it.

END